Stories from the Magic Kingdom

Patrick Kling
and
Kristen Waldbieser

Theme Park Press
The Happiest Books on Earth
www.ThemeParkPress.com

Theme Park Press publishes its books in a variety of print and electronic formats. Some content that appears in one format may not appear in another.

Editor: Bob McLain
Layout: Artisanal Text

ISBN 978-1-68390-142-6
Printed in the United States of America

Theme Park Press | www.ThemeParkPress.com
Address queries to bob@themeparkpress.com

Contents

Now Approaching Main Street Station

a Main Street story by Kristen Waldbieser

Do mi do so do so mi do, do mi do so...

The music poured out of the window, each note dancing on top of the cool, autumn breeze. The playful tune never lost its momentum, never missed a beat, and almost seemed to explain the beautiful morning that was occurring outside. Jack's shoulders gently swayed along as he passed by the open window, listening to the music that only his best friend could be playing. She had been there since sunrise, just to ensure she had time for a piano lesson before work.

Jack continued to walk up the street, watching the little town he'd spent his entire life in. Casey, the man that had given him his first job, was sweeping the front entrance of his famous hot dog shop, a favorite of everyone in town. A group of barbers sang a merry little tune as they set up their shop for their days' work. The sun was bright enough for Jack to tilt his hat down over his eyes, but the breeze was strong enough that it kept tilting it backwards. Maroon leaves danced around his feet, almost as if saying hello as they floated through the music-filled wind. He made his way over to the Main Street Bakery, his favorite stop in town, to pick up something sweet to start the morning with. He smiled as he was handed two small cakes with jam. He said his thanks, and walked out the door. It was just the start of another day.

Rounding the corner, he made his way back to the little window with the wonderful music pouring out of it. He stood under a lamppost and listened as each note greeted him.

"Emilee, focus your eyes on the keys. The piano isn't outside the window," Jack could hear Emilee's piano teacher say.

"Yes, Mr. Baker," Emilee responded.

Jack listened as the music continued, a beautiful jazzy tune that Emilee had been working on for months. She finished her arpeggios, the same ones Jack had heard her playing every Monday and Wednesday for as long as he could remember.

"Simply beautiful. However, I noticed you went a little off the melody around...." Mr. Baker began.

"I thought it could use a little change. The music takes my mind to far-off places," Emilee interrupted.

Jack smiled, laughing a bit to himself. It was such a typical answer from her. He heard the piano bench slide out against the hard wood floor, and could almost count the steps until Emilee would be in front of him. 3...2...1...

Her bright smile greeted him before any words could. She jumped off the second to last step, and skipped over to him, a warm hug used as her hello. Jack handed her one of the cakes.

"What's this for?" she asked, already taking a bite.

"Well, you're really quite exceptional. And any great musician deserves something for their efforts," he said. Her nose turned bright red. An odd quirk that she had. Instead of blushing, it was just her nose. She hated it, but Jack found it quite charming.

"Well, you know, I guess I am, aren't I?" she laughed, nudging him in the side. "Wait, were you listening again? I'm still working on that piece, it's really not ready to be heard yet."

"Well, then tell Mr. Baker to close the window during your lessons."

They began to walk down the street, enjoying their cakes, which Emilee had almost completely devoured. They watched as the same young men and women that they had gone to school with leapt on to the trolley that went up and down the street. The trolley was full of laughter and songs, as it was every day. The girls' dresses were all perfectly pressed, their petticoats just slightly peaking out from underneath. The boys all wore wide suspenders, not a flaw about them. They all looked as if they had stepped out of a painting. A few of them waved, and Jack and Emilee waved back at them. The usual courtesies.

After the trolley passed, they ran down their quaint Main Street, past the ice cream parlor and the dress shop. At the edge of the street, a small park waited for them, where even though the autumn leaves were falling, the grass remained green.

Jack and Emilee walked down to the park at the edge of Main Street practically every day. Away from the hubbub of their neighbors, they appropriately called it their "hub." Jack would often bring an ice cream cone or a sweet, something to make Emilee smile. Of all the places they had grown up visiting, the hub was their favorite. They sat down on the grass, staring out at the beautiful sky above them. However, Emilee's eyes drifted to the miles of trees in front of her.

"Do you ever wonder what's past those trees?" she asked him. Jack glanced over at her, then at the forest in front of them.

"Someone's been writing fantasy stories again," he said.

"Jack, I'm serious. Don't you ever think about if there's more than just the town we know?"

He had thought about it before, of course. When they were growing up, Emilee would spend hours telling Jack about the magical places that she imagined on the other side of those trees. But, others before them had ventured outward, only to find miles and miles of forest. And although those attempts had stopped over the years, Emilee's stories never did. And even though he'd heard them hundreds of times before, Jack never got tired of hearing Emilee tell her marvelous tales.

"So, what's it this time?" he asked.

"What if there was a place that we can't even begin to comprehend, because it's so far in the future? Maybe their waste bins come directly to you, or...." she began

"Do you want a waste bin with wheels on it? I could make that for you," Jack interrupted.

Emilee rolled her eyes. "It's just an *idea*, Jack."

They sat in silence. Jack looked over at Emilee, watching her eyes sparkle with curiosity. He always noticed that they seemed to shine more when she was deep in thought about the last place she had imagined. Whenever she told him about her latest idea, her smile would twist in to a smirk, and her brown eyes would almost glow with specks of green. Those were some of Jack's favorite moments, seeing her in her true element. And although he didn't really know how to talk to her about them, he enjoyed being the one that she told them to.

"I'm really on to something with my new locomotive model," Jack said, breaking the silence.

Jack worked as an engineer, tinkering on the train that connected the farms and homes on the outskirts of town with Main Street, the center of everything in their city. However, Jack's real passion was not fixing the old, but designing the new. He was always sketching out new models of streetcars, trolleys, and most importantly, trains. His dream was to create something that had never been done before. And between his passion to create a new machine, partnered with Emilee's dream to discover new places, they made a pretty good team.

"What's it going to do this time? Fly?" Emilee asked.

Jack smirked. "For your information, it might as well fly! With my new model, the train would be able to completely circle the entire city without having to stop *once*." He watched as Emilee raised her eyebrows. He could see the wheels turning in her head.

"Jack, that's impossible."

"Well, it's kind of fun to do the impossible."

"Do you think it'll work?" Her eyes sparkled even brighter.

"Well, that's the beauty of experimentation. We won't know until we try."

Emilee nudged him in the side, smiling. He always gave her such scientific answers like that, because he knew it always made her laugh. Jack smiled. *She really does have the best laugh*, he thought.

"Do you think it could...travel farther than just around the city?" Emilee asked.

He knew the question would come eventually. It was the same question she asked every time he shared a new development about the trains. He never knew how to answer her. He knew that he couldn't get the trains through that thick forest, not without years of work. And even if he could, he knew they would find what those before them had found. Nothing.

"Emilee, the track only runs in a circle on the perimeter of the city. To even try and build through that forest would be costly and dangerous. And to risk all that when there's nothing out there...." He hated being so blunt with her, but sometimes he just had to.

"We don't *know* there's nothing out there. We've been *told* there's nothing out there," she said, holding her ground. She never was one to give in.

"Well, let's see if I can get the locomotive around the city, and then we can go from there."

Emilee smiled, which made Jack smile as well.

"Aren't you going to be late for work?" Jack asked, looking down at his pocket watch. Emilee jumped up; Jack followed.

"No, no, no! If I'm late one more time, I'm getting reassigned to writing the help-wanted advertisements again," she said as they began racing toward town.

Emilee was a writer, a journalist for the *Main Street Gazette*. Wasting no time, they hopped on the trolley that had passed them by earlier. It was almost full. On one bench sat a small group of young men and women who were singing songs from the latest production that had been performed at their little Town Square Theater. On another, a husband and wife, clearly newlyweds, sat with their arms wrapped around each other, whispering and giggling. Across from Emilee and Jack sat a couple they had grown up with, Roger and Meg.

"Emilee, have you been rolling around in the dirt?" Meg snickered. Jack watched Emilee look down at her grass stained dress and her nose turned bright red.

Back when they were in school, Emilee was always applauded for her talents at the piano. On the other hand, Meg, who thought her singing talents were far beyond compare, was often overlooked. Meg's singing voice actually resembled the voice of a screaming cat, although no one would ever tell her that. Emilee looked over at Meg.

"Oh, you know me. I wasn't completely happy with the color of my dress, so I decided to take it upon myself to fix it! *Clearly,* you're just not up to date with the latest fashions."

Meg shrugged her shoulders, turning her back to them and facing Roger, her beau for who knows how long. Emilee tried to rub the grass stains off of her skirt, but she and Jack were quickly laughing at her failed efforts.

To no one's surprise, Meg quickly turned back around, always needing to have the last word. She was holding hands with Roger, who was smiling along.

"Emilee, has anyone asked you to join them at the autumn festival this weekend? You know there will be dancing and everything," Meg said.

Jack perked up at the mention of the festival. He had been meaning to ask Emilee to go with him for weeks, but he never knew how to start the conversation. And what if she said no? He worried that the chance of rejection would end the friendship that he couldn't do without.

"I'll be busy covering the festival for the *Gazette*," Emilee said.

Jack knew that was a lie. Emilee always told him what articles she had been assigned for the week, and the festival had never come up in conversation. That had to mean that no one had asked her yet.

"Well, isn't that a shame, then," Meg said, snickering and turning back toward Roger.

Jack thought about asking Emilee right there. It was a perfect opportunity. All he had to do was ask her to accompany him for the evening, as they knew they would have a wonderful time together. But, before he could find the words, the trolley slowed to a halt, and he watched Emilee hop off. He followed behind, walking with her to the corner and staring at the words stenciled on the window right above them: *The Main Street Gazette*.

"Meet me at the station after work, all right? I want to show you the new model," Jack said. Emilee nodded and gave her bright smile, before running up the stairs to her cozy office.

Emilee sat tapping her pencil against her desk, staring at the blank paper in front of her. She was supposed to be writing a piece on Mayor Weaver and the work he had done in the community lately. It would be a lovely piece, as long as she could get the words down. But her mind was elsewhere. She pulled a stack of papers out of her desk, where she kept all of the fantastic stories that she had written throughout the years.

She shuffled through the stack. Stories about worlds of fantasy, tales of adventure, and mysteries from the frontier. She loved writing about far-off places, the type that seemed to only exist in dreams. It wasn't that she didn't like her hometown; she really did. She loved spending her mornings before work with Jack at the hub, the festivals, all of it. But the idea of finding something *new*, and making a difference, pulled at her heart every minute.

Sighing, she put the stories back in her desk, and returned to the blank paper that stared up at her, planning out what she would write. She always had to write the same type of articles, week after week. An article on Fire Chief Smokey Miller, an interview with Beatrice Starr or Victoria Trumpetto. Each one just telling the same old story of someone else, never creating anything new.

"How's the article coming along?"

Emilee looked up to see her co-worker, Eli, leaning over her desk. Eli was the cartoonist for the paper. He was quite used to Emilee being off topic and often saw her hard at work on one of her stories, rather than the articles she was assigned. But then again, Emilee was quite used to Eli creating beautiful pieces of art that would never see the front page of the newspaper.

"Oh, you know, it's going to be an award-winner here," Emilee laughed, holding up the blank piece of paper in front of her.

"What is it that you're *really* working on, then?" he asked.

Emilee hesitated. Maybe, just maybe, he had the same thoughts. Perhaps someone else could envision the places that she imagined in her head. She shuffled through the papers on her desk, pulling out her latest fantasy story. She looked it over quickly, and then held it out in front of him.

"Just...don't laugh. It's not what we're used to," she said.

"That's my favorite kind of story."

Jack was writing down facts and figures, standing in the middle of the locomotive. He wanted to make sure every calculation was perfect this time. There was no room for error. Soon, he was interrupted by what sounded like a sing-song voice calling his name. He poked his head out the door, and sure enough he saw Emilee bouncing up the steps. He began to smile. He looked down at his pocket watch. It was only twelve o'clock.

"What are you doing here?" Jack laughed as Emilee reached the top of the stairs.

"I told them I was doing a little 'research' after lunch today. Which I am. I'm *researching* what's on the other side of that forest. And besides, I know it's so hard to be without me, isn't it?" she laughed.

Jack shook his head, even though he knew she was right.

"So, what are you up to?" she asked. She never was one to waste a single moment.

Jack pulled his notebook and pencil out of his pocket, and adjusted the glasses on his face. He glanced over the calculations on the page, making sure everything was perfect.

"Well, the original model of the locomotive, the one that we use around town currently, used a limited boiler with only one boiler tube. It could maybe only hold 3.7 liters of water in it. So, when the steam it created was piped through the cylinder and passed through the inlet valve, it didn't have enough pressure to get the piston moving for an extended period of time," Jack said, still looking over his notes.

"But when I tested the new model, I used four boiler tubes without accounting for the fact that the cylinder, *obviously*, would have to be enlarged by seventeen percent, or the piston would snap, and there wouldn't be any chance for reciprocating...."

"*Obviously*. Jack, I know you're trying to work this out, but perhaps use a little less technical gibberish?" Emilee was extremely intelligent, but she wasn't a mechanic like Jack was. His mind worked differently.

Jack thought completely in numbers and figures, dealing only in fact. Anything that couldn't be proven with a mathematical equation, well, it just couldn't be true. But his mind worked deliberately, constantly thinking of ways to improve his machines. Unfortunately, that meant that he did not realize how technical his speech was.

"I made sure that the big round thing was filled with the right amount of hot stuff. Is that better?"

"Much better," Emilee nodded.

She walked over to the locomotive that Jack had been working on for such a long time. He hadn't connected any of the passenger cars to it, and it looked much smaller than the *Roger E. Broggie* train that Emilee had grown up riding.

"Where's the train that's normally here? The one that circles the town?" she asked, looking at all the bells and whistles Jack had attached to this one.

"It's tucked away at the roadhouse until the festival, giving me time to really perfect this model."

Jack wrote down numbers in his notebook, but watched out of the corner of his eye as Emilee moved to the far edge of the platform. The wind tousled her brown hair as she stared out at the street ahead. Jack put his notebook down and walked over to her. He leaned on the railing next to her. From the top of the station, they could see the forest stretch farther than the eye could see.

"I suppose it could be possible," he finally said. Emilee looked over at him.

"The places you've written about for years. They could be possible. The dreams that you have, that I can't even fathom, maybe they're out there. I'm not quite sure how, but I suppose it takes curiosity to know for sure."

"Curiosity keeps leading us down new paths." That clever look was spread across her face. Determined, fierce, and inspired. Jack raised his eyebrows. He knew that look of hers.

"So let's find out what's out there," Jack said.

They jumped off the platform in front of the train, and walked along the tracks. Jack liked to check the first quarter of the tracks before he tried a new test to make sure there were no variables that could get in the way of his results. It was meticulous, but in his line of work, that's exactly what was needed.

Jack walked quickly, his eyes scanning the rails, checking for any broken parts or anything else that might slow the train. Emilee walked beside him, balancing herself on the rail.

"I think in my next story, I'll write about a far-off lagoon, but the only way to cross the lagoon is by braving a small bridge, high in the air. My explorer, desperate to see what's on the other side, makes her way across the rickety old bridge," she explained, walking backwards to tell Jack the tale.

"And then what will happen?" he asked her. Emilee face suddenly turned very serious.

"The unthinkable! She begins to lose her balance." Emilee began to sway back and forth on the rail. "Then down she goes! Tumbling toward certain doom!" Emilee laughed as she jumped down off the rail.

Her cry of *"Ow!"* snapped her out of her story.

Jack looked at her as she was putting all her weight on her left foot, slightly lifting the other above the ground. And although clearly in pain, her eyes were fixated right in front of her, staring at the ground.

"What did you do now?" Jack asked, used to Emilee jumping and falling off the tracks.

"Jack, look," she said, still staring straight ahead of her.

"What are you talking about?"

She pointed to the ground in front of her. Jack pulled his glasses closer to his eyes and looked at the grass. He looked up at her, completely confused about what had so entranced her.

"Emilee, there's nothing there."

Emilee looked over at him, her eyebrows scrunched together. She looked back down at the ground, then back up at him again.

"You're joking, right? You're telling me you can't see it?"

"See what? There's nothing there but grass."

Emilee bent forwards and put her hand down. It seemed to stop a few inches before it reached the ground. She grabbed Jack's hand, holding it tightly, and pulled him down next to her. Jack looked over at her, his eyes wide. He held on to her hand, but she quickly moved his hand down and placed it where hers had been just a moment ago.

He felt the cold metal underneath his hand, although as he looked out in front of him, his hand was resting on air. He pulled his hand back, falling backwards.

"What was that?!"

"You're telling me you don't see that track heading off in to the trees?!" Emilee asked.

Jack didn't know how to answer. Still staring at the ground in front of him, there was nothing, but he couldn't deny feeling the rail, as if it really was there. And how would Emilee have known it was there if she hadn't really seen it? His mind raced, full of questions that he didn't have the answers to, a feeling he couldn't stand.

"How far does it go?" he managed to ask.

"You really don't see it?"

Jack shook his head.

"It goes under the trees, straight into the forest."

Emilee stood up, Jack right behind her. She stepped up on the track, and it appeared to Jack that she was walking on air. Jack followed her and felt the hard surface beneath his feet, though it looked as if he stood inches above the ground. He swayed back, but Emilee grabbed his hand to keep him steady. She moved forward, pushing through the trees and bushes in front of them, and holding on to his hand to lead the way. Jack held on to her tightly, hoping she wouldn't notice that his palms were starting to sweat.

They pulled apart branches and leaves, climbed through thorns, trying to see where this track would go. But the longer they traveled, the more the shrubbery seemed to increase. Emilee kept pushing forward, watching for any change in scenery, anything at all, but it just seemed to get darker and greener as they continued on.

"We can't keep at this all night. It could go on for miles," Jack finally said, attempting to sit on the rails that he still couldn't see. Emilee sat down next to him.

"We can't just stop, Jack. This is... I mean, this track just *magically* appeared out of nowhere!"

"There has to be some sort of explanation for this, some sort of reasoning behind it. No denying it's there, but why can't it be seen?" He began trying to work everything out in his head. Emilee stared him straight in the eyes.

"Jack, not everything comes down to facts and figures. Sometimes things can't be explained through reasoning. You just have to trust your instincts."

Jack pulled his notepad out of his pocket. He looked at his notes and calculations, all perfectly pieced together to make sense. He flipped through, looking for something he might have missed.

"It doesn't matter if you can see it or not. It's here. And finding this.... Jack, this is the adventure I've wanted my entire life. The *discovery* you've been dreaming of your entire life. We have to see how far this can take us."

Jack paused for a moment. It was true, this was the type of discovery he had always dreamed of. He wanted to make a difference. He picked up a small rock off the ground, and threw it in front of him. He heard the loud *clang* as it bounced off the invisible track and back to the ground.

"All right. But we don't even know if a train will run on a track like this. Let alone through all the trees," he mumbled.

"Come on, Jack, you're telling me you're going to let some trees stop you?"

"I suppose I could attach a device to the front of the train that could clear away all of this. It might lessen the distance we can go, because it'll require a lot more force, but it might work. If this track can even support the weight of the train. It might work."

"*Might* is a pretty good place to start."

"Well, then, what are we waiting for?" he said with a wink.

They turned around, Emilee pulling Jack closely behind her. Jack felt like he was flying, watching his feet run inches above the ground. Emilee looked back at him, her brown eyes now sparkling with green, bursting with excitement.

They approached the part of the rail that Jack could see, the same circle that he had navigated more times than he could count. Emilee halted in her tracks, causing Jack to stumble behind her. Without saying a word, she pulled her ribbon out of her hair and tied it to the branch right next to her. Its bright blue color almost seemed to glow against the dark green tree.

"With that track going under these bushes, it would be difficult to see it from the inside of the train. At least if I see that bright blue ribbon, it'll give us an indicator of where to stop."

Jack raised his eyebrows quickly. He hadn't thought of that. Before he could acknowledge her quick thinking, she was already racing off toward the station, ready to begin their adventure.

They ran up the stairs to the top of the station where the train sat. It stared back at them, ready to take on the challenges they were about to face. Jack ran up to it, checking every bolt and wheel, ensuring everything was in top condition. Emilee watched as he wiped his glasses on his shirt, cleaning off some dust that had collected.

"Jack, come on! Let's go! Let's *go!*" Emilee yelled in delight, catching Jack's smile as he turned around. She didn't want to waste a moment.

"Almost ready. Let me just make sure that the ratio from coal to water is perfect, otherwise...."

"Oh, just *hurry*," she said with a wink.

Jack quickly hopped inside the train, writing down notes as fast as his pencil could take him. Emilee walked over to the far side of the platform and stared out ahead of her, just as she had earlier in the day. It was funny, she had looked down that same street only a few hours earlier, but it looked different now.

"All aboard," Jack shouted, poking his head out of the door. Emilee turned around, jumping into the locomotive.

They stood next to each other, and Emilee felt her heart racing faster and faster. She grabbed on to Jack's hand, and this time, not just to pull him along. Jack looked over at her and smiled. He squeezed her hand tightly.

"Here we go...." With the sound of a whistle, they were off.

The train went along smoothly, and Jack piloted it perfectly. Emilee stared ahead, watching as the trees whizzed past them. It wouldn't take long to reach the part of the track that they had flagged with Emilee's hair ribbon.

"Now, remember, we're just seeing if it can support the weight of the train. If it does, then I'll attach some sort of blade to the cowcatcher to clear off the trees. But no sense in doing that if this new track won't hold the train."

"And why wouldn't a track hold the train?" Emilee asked.

"Why would a track appear invisible?"

Emilee sighed. Jack believed that the track was really there. He touched it. However, Emilee thought it might be what was beyond the track that Jack couldn't wrap his head around.

A few feet ahead of them, Emilee spotted her blue ribbon dancing on the cool breeze. Jack saw it, too, and slowed the train down. As the train got slower and slower, Emilee's heart beat faster and faster.

"It's's a bit of a sharp turn here, so hold on to something tightly and hopefully I won't flip this thing over." Even though he was laughing, Emilee knew that a part of him might have been serious.

"Here goes nothing," he whispered to himself.

Emilee clenched a rod tightly as the train began to turn at an angle it had never turned before. The wheels screeched against the rails as Jack inched it forward and pulled back on the brakes simultaneously. However loud and difficult, the train turned exactly where it needed to go.

"Jack! We're doing it! You're doing it!" Emilee cheered. Jack smiled.

"Ok, now I'm just going to ease...."

Before he could continue, the train slammed to a halt, sending Jack and Emilee flying toward the front of the locomotive. Emilee struggled to regain her breath. They sat up, slowly, staring at each other.

"Did you do that?" Emilee whispered, as her voice wouldn't carry any louder.

"No, I was sending it forward," Jack said, slowly getting to his feet.

"Did we fall? Did the track not hold?"

Jack didn't answer; he was too busy looking at the controls of the train, seeing what could have caused such an abrupt stop. Emilee got to her feet, and looked out in front of her. The train sat perfectly still, resting on the tracks leading in to the forest.

"Emilee, the train is still floating in the air!" Emilee hadn't even noticed that Jack had left the train, and was now examining the track below.

Emilee realized that Jack still couldn't see the track, but clearly it was there, as a train of that size, or any size, couldn't simply float above the ground. Jack joined her in the train again, putting his notebook back in his pocket.

"I've added some more coal. I think what might have happened is that the turn took a lot more power than I had accounted for," Jack said in his matter-of-fact way.

"So, we'll keep moving forward, then?"

"We keep moving forward."

Emilee watched as Jack pulled levers and brought the locomotive back to life. The whistle filled their silence, and the sound of the wheels turning echoed against it. Emilee waited for the locomotive to begin moving. Seconds passed, although they felt like minutes, and no movement. Jack continued to pull at levers and push others forward, frantically moving from one to the other. Still, no matter what he did, no movement.

"What's going on?" Emilee asked.

"I...I don't know. It should be working. There's no reason that it's not moving forward. I don't understand...." Jack said, shaking his head as he tried everything he could to get the train to move again.

The sound of the engine was louder and louder, and the wheels were screeching against the iron rails yet again, turning faster and faster. But as fast as they went, and as loud as it was, they never moved in inch.

"Jack! Stop!" Emilee screamed, noticing smoke coming from the wheel below.

Emilee noticed the wheels beginning to slow, and the smoke fade away. The sound of the engine was now silent, and everything seemed to calm down for a moment.

"What just happened?" Emilee asked.

She looked over at Jack, who was frantically writing down notes and shaking his head. He mumbled to himself, but Emilee couldn't quite make out what he was saying. Finally, he was able to speak.

"I've never seen anything like that before. The train was running. Everything was working perfectly, we just couldn't move. Not an inch."

"Why?" Emilee asked.

Jack shook his head. "I don't know."

Jack never said that he didn't know something. He would usually come up with some sort of hypothesis as to what was happening. But to admit that he had no idea, Emilee knew this truly was something he had never experienced before.

Jack jumped down. He checked every part of the locomotive meticulously, looking for any sort of variable he may have missed. Emilee jumped down, standing next to him.

"You still don't see that track, do you?" she asked.

"No, Emilee, I don't. I can't deny that it's there. I just don't understand how it's possible. Or why it's there," he said.

He leaned up against the train, cleaning off his glasses with the corner of his shirt. Emilee leaned next to him. She watched as he cleaned the glasses over and over, clearly deep in thought and not at all focused on the smudge he had missed four times already.

"So what do we do now?" Jack asked. He placed his glasses back on his nose and looked over at her.

"We try again. We *have* to try again."

"Then we'll try again," Jack said, his smile returning.

Emilee smiled in return, with determination in her eyes. This wasn't over. They couldn't give up, not yet. Not when they were so close. Jack jogged to the front of the train and knelt down next to the wheel.

"Look, the front wheel of the train is resting on the...*new* track. It's holding it up without a problem. But why won't it move even an inch forward. It hasn't reached the trees yet. Emilee, is there something I am not seeing on the rail?" he asked, inspecting every detail.

"Nothing," Emilee said as she knelt down in front of the train.

"Maybe it will require more pressure. Perhaps there is some sort of resistance on this track that is causing the halt...." Jack mumbled to himself as he wrote down some notes.

"Should we try again with more steam?" She didn't really understand the mechanics behind steam engines, but it sounded like a good guess.

"We'll try as many times as it takes," Jack said.

"Well, then, let's quit talking and begin doing."

"Emilee, wake up," Jack said, as he tapped on her shoulder.

Emilee stirred awake, sitting up from the hot floor of the locomotive that she had fallen asleep on. Her eyes were tired, and she clearly struggled to open them. Her hair had fallen in front of her face. Jack had never seen it in such disarray before. He smiled. *She still looked beautiful*, he thought.

"We've been working all night," Jack mumbled, still trying to wake himself up.

"I don't even remember falling asleep," Emilee said, yawning.

They sat still for a moment. They had worked straight through the night. Jack was constantly making adjustments, like the quantity of water, or the amount of coal. Emilee ran from one end to the locomotive to the other, assisting Jack with any task she could. But every time they tried to inch forward, they were met with the same screeching of the wheels but not an inch forward. Nothing.

"We're still stuck, aren't we?" She knew the answer.

"We're still stuck," Jack said.

They sat next to each other, looking straight ahead.

"Emilee, we have to get this train moving again. We either get it moving forward to who knows where, or we get it moving back. It's blocking the track around the city, so the other train won't be able to get around it. With the festival this weekend, if that train isn't able to get people into town, I'll lose my job."

Emilee nodded. They had to figure this out quickly. Emilee wondered how long this mysterious track would even be around for. After all, if it could appear invisible, who was to say it couldn't vanish completely?

"Wait...work! Jack, what time is it?!" Emilee gasped, and suddenly realized that she couldn't sit and reflect any longer.

Jack pulled out his pocket watch, and his eyes grew wider as he read the time. Late.

"8:50," he said quickly.

Emilee jumped up. She brushed off her dress and pulled her hair back behind her. She wouldn't have time to go home and change her dress before work.

"Jack, I need your vest," she said.

Jack handed it over without hesitation. She fastened the vest, hoping it would change the appearance of her dress enough to avoid any questions from her colleagues.

They ran back to the station as fast as they could. Jack laughed a bit as Emilee almost tripped over another part of the track as she always did. They rounded the corner, and soon found themselves racing down the stairs from the station to Main Street. The chiming of the clock from Town Hall rang out, signaling the start of the work day.

"I'll go to Town Hall this morning, explain that there's, well, *something* blocking the track, so it's best that the trains not run today. Meet me back at the station after work," Jack said.

Emilee gave Jack a hug goodbye, wrapping her arms around his neck tightly. Jack gave her a squeeze, taking in the moment for as long as it would last. Far too quickly, she was off, running in the opposite direction toward the *Gazette*.

Jack turned and faced Town Hall. It was never a good conversation when he had to explain that the train would be out of operation for the day. Lectures on inconvenience and disappointment on the train being down were sure to fill his morning. There would be complaints on how long families had been waiting to ride the train, and how it completely ruined their week. He had planned exactly what he would say to the mayor. A large tree had fallen in the middle of the night, and it would take the day to clear it. *Yes, that would work perfectly,* he thought to himself.

He walked through the door, mumbling to himself how he would start the conversation. He may have been brilliant, but he wasn't always articulate with his words. As he walked in, he found that the office was abuzz. Everyone was hard at work preparing for the weekend's festivities.

Behind him, one of Emilee's co-workers walked through the door. Jack had met him a few times, but he didn't know him well.

"Hello, Jack," Eli said, approaching him.

"Hello, Elias." They quickly shook hands.

"Right. You and Emilee are pretty close, aren't you?" Eli asked.

"I'd say so," Jack said.

"She's really something. I mean, you're close with her, so of course you know that. But her imagination is just unbelievable. She's really something."

Jack didn't know what to say. Of course he knew that. He had known that since they were children. But to hear it from someone else? Well, it made him nervous.

"I was wondering.... Do you know if anyone has asked to escort her to the festival this weekend?"

Jack froze. No, he hadn't asked her yet, but he was going to. Wasn't he? Doubts filled his mind, wondering if Emilee would prefer to go with Eli, the charismatic cartoonist who seemed to understand her creative mind.

"I...um, I think so."

Eli's smile faded. "Oh. Of course she is. Well, I suppose I can only hope that it doesn't go well, and there will be another chance!" Eli laughed. Jack pretended to laugh along with him.

Eli shuffled through the stack of papers in his hand. Jack looked as he saw many different posters for the festival, featuring different parts of their town. Eli had captured the essence of the town perfectly.

"Oh, don't mind these. Just posters. But this...." he began as he pulled one of the papers toward the front. "Has she shown you any of her stories? I read the fantasy story that she always seems to be reading. I couldn't help but illustrate it. I didn't want to leave it on my desk. I couldn't risk her seeing it without me there."

At first, Jack didn't want to look at it. He was jealous that Emilee had shown someone else the stories that she liked to keep so private. He had always thought that her stories were something kept between the two of them, something special that they shared. Why did she share them in Eli? *Was* she interested in Eli, and had just never mentioned it? Jack was pulled out of his thoughts as he looked at the drawing in front of him. It was filled with whimsy and color, just as Emilee had described it to him. A grand castle sat in the middle of the picture, surrounded by colorful buildings and welcoming cottages.

"You're right. She is something," Jack said, looking intently at the picture.

"You know, I think it's quite possible for a place like this to exist. Don't you?"

"I suppose it could be possible, I don't really know for sure," Jack mumbled, his eyes still glued to the picture.

"Well, why not? You could reach the stars if you just believe. So why couldn't you find a place where every wish could come true? At least, that's what Emilee wrote," Eli said. He handed Jack Emilee's story, along with the picture.

"Believe in her. Believe in *this*," Eli said. And with a nod of his hat, he was gone.

"Don't leave without me!" Emilee yelled as she ran up the stairs to the station.

Jack laughed, which made his glasses slide down his nose a bit. He used the end of his pencil to push them back up, something that always made Emilee smile.

She sat down next to him, and looked the figures that he had written in his notebook. She could tell he had been hard at work, as the handwriting was absolutely horrible. His penmanship seemed to get worse and worse the farther into a project he got.

"Now, Ms. Emilee, I believe we have an adventure ahead of us," Jack said, gesturing his hand toward the track. She laughed, stepping up onto the rails.

Emilee could feel her heart beating in her chest. She just *knew* it would work this time, but the determined look in Jack's eyes was something she had not seen before.

"So, I saw your friend Eli today," he began.

"Yes, he told me you two ran into each other!"

Jack raised his eyebrows. "What are your...thoughts on him?"

Emilee hesitated for a moment, grinning. It was curious. Jack had never asked her *thoughts* on someone before.

"He's great. An extremely talented artist, a master of his craft," she said, smirking.

"He is. The posters he designed for the festival were excellent, I must admit. You know.... I think he wanted to ask you to the festival."

He wasn't sure why he told her that. What if she was overjoyed at the thought of going with him? Then what would he do?

"Is that so?" Emilee asked with a mischievous look on her face.

"Just what I heard." Jack paused., "So.... Would you go with him? If he asked?"

"Jack, there's only one man in town that I would ever *consider* going to the festival with," she said, looking up at him with her brown and green eyes.

"Oh? Who's that?"

"You really haven't figured this one out yet?" she said, grabbing his hand.

He squeezed her hand back and smiled. His smile was so wide, Emilee was almost sure his glasses would be knocked off his face. They continued walking hand in hand, taking in the moment.

"What is it that you're looking for out there? Why do you want to leave so badly?"

Emilee paused for a moment. "I just…. I know there's something more. Something different. There's a story worth telling out there, and I want to find it. I don't want to be the same as every other person before me. I want to make a change."

"Then that's exactly what you'll do."

"That's exactly what *we'll* do," she corrected him.

Their conversation was put to a halt as they stood with the locomotive sitting in front of them in the same location as where they had left it.

"I went ahead and rigged a few axes to the front of the cow-catcher that will move along with the wheels. So, theoretically, if we move forward, the locomotive itself will clear the trees away," he explained as they walked around to the front of the train.

"You still don't see that track, do you?"

Jack didn't answer. He didn't know how to answer. He could already see the disappointment in her eyes, wishing he could see things the way she did. He pulled out his notebook and looked at all his numbers. Surely, it had to make sense somewhere.

Emilee walked over to him and smacked the notebook out of his hand. Jack looked up at her, still unsure of what to say.

"Jack! Not everything has to come down to numbers and logic! Sometimes you just have to *believe* in something. Truly believe, not just because I want you to. Some things are beyond calculations."

She bent down to pick the notebook up. As she did, she noticed a colorful piece of paper sticking out the top.

"What's that?" She asked, handing the notebook back to Jack.

Jack opened the notebook to the page, looking at the drawing that Eli had given him earlier, carefully placed on top of Emilee's story. Emilee's eyes grew wide, her smile growing even more. The two of them stared at the picture, Jack's eyes scanning every inch of it. He saw in the corner of the picture a small railroad leading up behind the castle. *Could that possibly be the same track we're standing in front of?* he thought to himself. As he leaned in to look closer at the picture, Emilee grabbed on to his hand.

Jack stumbled, tripping over his feet and falling on his back.

"Now what did you do that for?" Emilee asked, laughing. Jack's eyes were glued in front of him.

"I see it! Emilee, the track! It's right there!"He began to write notes as quickly as he could.

"I don't understand. Why can you see it now, when just a moment ago you couldn't? What's changed?" She asked as she watched Jack jump up and carefully examine the track.

"Emilee, I never understood the places you were trying to reach. And I was so afraid that if you found it, you would be gone. I convinced myself that it was impossible, that the legends we knew had to be true. But I believe there's a way to go on this adventure. And I want to be the one to take this adventure with you."

Emilee wrapped her arms around his neck, overwhelmed with excitement. Jack grabbed her hands and began pulling her toward the door of the locomotive.

"Come on. Now's the time!" He pulled at levers and brought the train to life.

"Are you ready for this adventure?" Emilee asked, beaming from ear to ear.

Jack nodded, holding his breath as he attempted to inch the train forward. To their surprise, it responded. Slowly, the train pushed through the trees in front of them, following the rail that they hoped would lead to their wildest dreams.

"It's working, Jack! It's working!"

Emilee looked out the door as the trees began to pass by, faster and faster. And although the trees continued to keep coming and coming and coming, she waited until something would put an end to the forest that she had known her entire life.

"What do you think is really out there?" she asked, her eyes glued towards the horizon.

"It's hard to say. Maybe we'll find a far-off lagoon with a rickety old bridge. Or maybe a place where waste bins can move all on their own!"

"Jack, I'm *serious*!" She laughed with him.

"I think that as long as we can get past these trees, anything you can possibly imagine is out there," he said.

Emilee suddenly stopped laughing. "What do you mean *as long as...?*"

"Well, this engine can only go for about five hours. We don't know how far this forest will last."

Emilee hadn't thought of that. What if there was nothing but forest forever, and they had now trapped themselves with no way back? Or what if the land that was out there wasn't the beautiful fantasy that she had imagined, and they could never return home?

"Well, if I'm going to risk everything for someone, it wouldn't be anyone but you," Jack said, grabbing Emilee's hand.

They continued on, hand in hand, waiting to see what awaited them beyond the forest. An hour passed, and still all they saw were trees. Emilee's excitement continued to mix with worry, causing her to squeeze Jack's hand tighter with every mile they traveled. Another hour, and they still saw nothing but trees. Jack slowed the train as they went, hoping to conserve as much energy as he could. Two-and-a-half hours, and Emilee spotted something up in the distance.

"Jack...look!"

The sun was shining through the trees, which reflected off the metal rails on the ground. However, this track did not seem to follow one straight line any more. Instead, it split off in five different directions. Jack brought the train's engine down, slowing it to a stop.

They stepped out of the locomotive, looking at the tracks in front of them. As they looked ahead, even the color and types of trees seemed to change. They were a more brilliant green, matched with a sky filled with vivid pinks and purples. Jack was in awe, taking in the beautiful sight. But it was the look on Emilee's face, the pure excitement in her eyes mixed with a deep sense of wonder, that he couldn't keep his eyes off of.

They looked over at each other, both in disbelief of what was in front of them. Emilee had dreamed they could potentially find one unique place, but now they had five potential uncertainties ahead. Could they see them all? Emilee's mind raced with the possibilities.

"What do we do now?" Jack asked.

"We pick one," she said, as if it were just as simple as that.

"Just pick one?" Jack said with with a laugh.

"We have no idea what lies at the end of any of these tracks. We're just going off of pure instinct. So, take a breath, don't think about it, just pick one."

Jack did as he was told. He took in a deep breath, closed his eyes for a moment, and pointed in front of him.

"That's the one, then?" Emilee asked with a smile.

"That's the one."

They stepped aboard the locomotive, and Jack brought the train back to life and looked ahead of them. Emilee's eyes were almost completely green.

"Wait a minute...." Jack began.

Emilee's smile faded quickly. "What? Is something wrong?"

"Well, it's just...I have a date for the festival this weekend, and who knows if I'll make it back in time!"

Emilee shook her head and smiled.

Jack pulled Emilee close, brushing the strand of hair out of her eyes, and pulled her in to kiss her. She kissed him back, feeling as if she had filled in a part of her story that she had been missing for far too long.

"Off we go," Jack said, as the whistle rang out through the air.

The trees flashed past them as they moved faster and faster down the unknown path. Hand in hand, they smiled as they kept moving forward. Off in the distance, the silhouette of a castle could be seen peaking above the trees. Emilee smiled, knowing that this was only the beginning of a great adventure.

Jungle Navigation Co. Episode LXXI

a Adventureland story by Patrick Kling

"As we approach the dock, please make sure you keep your hands and arms inside the boat at all times. We wouldn't want to hurt...the dock. We hope you had an outstanding cruise with us here. Pretty soon you'll be *out standing*, on the dock...."

A girl screamed.

"What is that?!" a man shouted.

"It's a man floating on a tree limb!"

"*Wood* you look at that folks, this is in*tree*guing. I'm in disbe*leaf*. We need to get to the *root* of the this," the Skipper continued. He leaned over a bit closer, as his boat approached the tree limb. "*Wooden* you know! It's Skipper Andrew," he said as he flipped the throttle into reverse, halting the boat.

He was two feet away from Andrew, yet he took out a megaphone and shouted.

"You need some help?!"

Andrew was unresponsive.

"Nothing to worry about here, folks. You can go ahead and *leaf* now. We'll take care of our friend. *Walnut* let this stand. We'll make sure to *spruce* him up, *oak*-ay?"

The Jungle Cruise passengers chuckled and departed the boat, thinking it was all a part of the act. The Jungle Navigation Co. was known for their shenanigans, quickness, and humor on their various tour offerings, but this time it wasn't.

The Skipper, named Allen, took out his radio.

"Harbor Master, this is the *Mongala Millie*. We have a bit of a situation. Andrew appears to have floated up on a branch. Also, I'm going to need a hot towel in about 90 seconds." Without skipping a beat, Allen jumped into the water, grabbed

Andrew, and pulled him onto the dock. He has a pulse, but his breathing is unresponsive.

"Wake up, *rook*," he said, laughing. A few other skippers gathered around.

"What happened?"

"Probably had a few too many at the canteen last night."

They all laughed, except Skipper Adam. Adam liked to take it upon himself to guide new recruits. The Jungle Navigation Training manual said a lot of things, but not about how to make it in this remote outpost. He'd been there for many years and seen many unexplainable things.

Allison, the ruthless, loose cannon of the outpost, dumped a bucket of water on Andrew, who immediately woke up and screamed.

"Where am I? Where is my boat? What happened?! Am I alive? Is this hell? What's the meaning of life?"

"Looks like you partied a little too hard last night. You look okay, though. We found you washed up on the dock," Allen said.

"No, no, no, I was on a boat. We entered the Cambodian temple and...and...a whirlpool opened up! I...I- don't know... what happened next. We must have been...." Andrew began.

"Enough! Get this rook to the barracks," Allison barked.

"No, we need to save my passengers!" Andrew pleaded.

Adam led Andrew to his tent. The tent was simple. Two hammocks, a bureau they shared, and a few posters along the walls. Andrew's prized possession was a poster of Charlie Chaplin, his all time favorite comedian. Andrew grew up watching Chaplin in theaters when he was younger. As an adult he knew he wanted to work in comedy. At a very young age, his parents took him to Africa on a tour by the Jungle Navigation Co. Ever since then, he wanted to work for them. He would have started working for them when he was a kid, but the Jungle Navigation Co. had strict labor policies restricting the emlpoyment of chlidren. Mostly due to the additional nap time that would've been required beyond that of a normal adult.

Adam's space on the bureau was quite a bit different. Most of his drawers were filled with dystopian literature such as *It Can't Happen Here* and *Brave New World*. Each book was heavily

annotated. Words and phrases circled, scribbled out, and there
were nonsensical notes written throughout. One drawer con-
tained his grooming kit for his handlebar mustache. It was
part of his signature look. His wardrobe was smaller than the
others. Literally. He preferred tank tops when not in uniform,
showing off his Masonic tattoos and nihilistic phrases. His
prized tattoo was an all-seeing eye located across his chest.
Uniform policies were strict at the Jungle Navigation Co., but
they had recently loosened up their mustache policy, and Adam
immediately grew out a full handlebar. He played fast and loose
with the policies, though. As soon as he'd depart the outpost on
a Jungle Cruise tour, he would rip off his company-mandated
long-sleeve shirt, letting his tank top do the work.

"Get some rest. Dr. Marley should return in less than an
hour. We will sort it out then. I have dock duty," Adam stated
as he left the tent.

Andrew laid there in the hammock recounting the last 24
hours. *Was it all a dream?* He remembered the moments leading
up to it so vividly. While he was new, it was still a route he had
navigated a few times before. They had just entered the temple
when *it* happened.

Meanwhile, back at the dock Allen checked in with Adam.

"How is the rook recovering? Some people just can't handle
the Canteen."

"I believe him. We need to figure this thing out," Adam
replied.

"You can't possibly believe this nonsense...."

"You know weird things happen out in the Jun...." Adam
said, growing frustrated. The loudspeaker interrupted.

"Skipper Andrew, please report to Dr. Marley's office. Also,
to the skipper who was driving the *Mongala Millie*, you left
your lights on."

"Dang it, I *always* do that," Allen said.

"Cover for me, I got to go with him," Adam proclaimed.

"Cover for *me*, I need go turn off the lights on the boat."

Andrew and Adam entered the outpost management office
located on the second floor of the Skipper Canteen. Here, Dr.
Marley ran the place. Dr. Marley was a well groomed, calm,
cool, and collected leader. His uniform was ironed and pressed

daily, a rather painstaking chore for his assistant, Johnny. He donned a breakfast monocle on his left eye, as he did every morning. His office was full of pictures of his prior adventures in the jungle. His prized possession was a colorful, tribal mask that he and Lord Henry Mystic were given when he was a younger skipper. Lord Henry, a frequent passenger, was quite the collector. He was able to communicate, bargain, and win over anyone. But that's a story for another time.

"Look, boys, take a seat and tell me all about what happened," Dr. Marley stated sympathetically.

"W-w-well, yesterday, I was entering the Cambodian shrine and suddenly a whirlpool formed.... I don't remember anything after that. Next thing I know I was woken up on the dock by Allen," Andrew said.

"Look, boys, some are claiming you simply had a bit too much fun at the Skipper Canteen last night. These are serious accusations," Dr. Marley replied as he removed his monocle.

"It's the honest truth, sir. We *must* find those passengers. I need to leave right now!" Andrew shouted.

"Let's figure this out.... If a boat and a gaggle of passengers are missing, we should know. Johnny, can you please run down to the dock and grab the master log, post haste." He gave his monocle a quick wipe and then placed it onto his right eye.

Johnny left the office. For a moment, Andrew was nervous. Was this all a dream? His memories were so vivid for the tour. He had been out for hours with them before reaching the temple. He remembered the passengers of the boat, an eccentric businessman and his mistress, a family of four, and a few frequent travelers who heckled him.

"I believe him, sir," Adam stated confidently.

"Yeah," Dr. Marley said as he removed his monocle, "you'll believe anything."

Johnny returned with the master log. He set it on Dr. Marley's desk and a plume of dust burst from the binder. Dr. Marley gave the binder a big blow causing dust to fill the air. He coughed profusely.

"*This* looks promising," Dr. Marley quipped. He took out his bifocals and opened the binder. Two massive cockroaches flew from a nook within. He glanced over several pages.

"Hhhmmm…. This dang thing hasn't been updated in 10 years!"

He threw the log back at Johnny. Another cockroach fled from inside it, and walked up Johnny's arm. Johnny shrieked.

"Look, boys, we have no record of which boats are out on tour from this outpost, and we definitely have *no* idea if we have a horde of missing passengers," Dr. Marley began. He looked over at his trusty assistant.

"Johnny, would you please excuse us for a moment."

Johnny closed his eyes and stuck his fingers in his ears and began to hum. Dr. Marley removed his bifocals and placed his monocle onto his left eye.

"Look, boys, I've seen some interesting things out in that jungle. I'd even go as far as to call them *mystical*."Adam's eyes glowed and he grinned from ear to ear. Dr. Marley continued in a wistful tone as he look out the window of his office.

"Back when I was a young skipper like yourselves, my good friend Timothy went missing," he said, removing his monocle.

"His last-known location was over near that temple. He was out on a scouting mission attempting to find new passageways for our tours. But most importantly, he was attempting to find a type of apple we all liked. He was a hero. We conducted many searches. Management at the time gave up, figuring he had been eaten by an animal, or worse. I never believed it. Timothy always had his wits about him. I think something happened at that temp…."

"Le-let me go back to that temple. Adam and I will go out there and figure this out," Andrew said. Dr. Marley stared out the window for a few more moments, placing his monocle on his right eye. He slammed his hand on the window sill.

"Look, boys, I'll give you a chance. We can't let this get out, we could lose business. We could lose everything. Go find out what happened, find the passengers, and most importantly, find that boat. It isn't insured." He removed the monocle.

"Thank you, sir, we won't let you down," Adam said.

"*Johnny*, get back in here!" Dr. Marley shouted, as he grabbed Johnny's finger out of his right ear.

"We're assembling a team to go figure this out. Who do we have in the outpost at the moment?"

Johnny looked at his pocket watch. "Looks like the only other skippers available are Allen and Allison."

"Andrew, Adam, Allen, and Allison, eh? We should stop scheduling the skippers alphabetically. Okay, Johnny, go let them know they will leave immediately. Also, let's start using that dang master log, and for Petes' sake do something about those cockroaches."

"Right away, sir."

Dr. Marley grabbed Adam and Andrew by the shoulder and whispered in their ears. "One more thing, fellas, keep an eye out for those apples."

Adam and Andrew headed toward the door. Dr. Marley turned towards them.

"Wait, one more thing, Adam...." He placed his monocle on his left eye and raised his eyebrow. "Put a dang shirt on."

Andrew and Adam were relieved and validated. This could be one heck of a journey for them. Adam was also relieved he was able to be shirtless for the entire meeting. Adam gave Andrew a firm look.

"I promise to you that we will not rest until we find your lost boat, okay? Now let's grab some lunch."

They walked downstairs to the Skipper Canteen to have lunch. The canteen crowd was boisterous during shift change and late evenings. Many cruises lasted for days on end, so the canteen was a place for skippers to blow off some steam and escape the tourists. Things had been a bit more lively recently, as word had come down from the head office that beer, wine, and a few other libations would be allowed to be served. Deep in the heart of the jungle, beer and wine was safer to drink than water. Adam and Andrew grabbed some grub and sat at their usual table.

The door of the canteen slammed open. It was Allison, with Allen trailing behind.

"Where are they?!" she bellowed into the room.

She locked eyes with Andrew.

"There he is! That rookie scum." The canteen fell silent. She marched toward Andrew and Adam's table, stomping her feet and knocking over chairs.

"News travels fast here," Adam quipped.

"Who do you think you are? You've barely been here a day. You party too hard last night and start making up stories. Now you've roped us into some silly, reckless mission into the dark depths of the jungle."

"That's enough," Allen piped up.

Allison was the renegade. In prior years, she'd been a safari guide for another faction of the company over at the Harambe Wildlife Reserve. She was transferred after she got a bit too trigger happy during a safari. Well, quite a few safaris. Any other employee would have been fired, but her grandfather had been a life-long friend of Albert Falls, the late founder of the Jungle Navigation Co. Alberta Falls, Albert's granddaughter, had honored her grandfather's agreement to keep Allison employed. When she was transferred to the Jungle Cruise, division management made the decision to take away the onboard pistols to avoid any further "incidents."

"Allison, I'll have you know that we have no record of Andrew being here last night. So take your accusations elsewhere," bartender Alex said, peering over the table.

With a large grunt, Allison headed to her favorite table on the other side of the canteen.

Alex continued to talk with Andrew and Adam.

"Come to think of it, we don't have any records of anyone doing anything anywhere. We should really look into having better record keeping."

"Today, Allison verbally attacked Andrew," Alex said, grabbing a napkin and a pencil to take notes.

"There we go," he said as he pinned the napkin to the backboard of the bar.

"Well, fellas, I don't know what happened out there, but I'll be behind you every step of the way. I'll also do what I can to keep an eye on Allison," Allen said.

"Thanks," Adam replied.

"Now listen, rook. You don't know Allison very well, but here's my advice. It may take awhile for her to warm up to you, but when she does, she'll have your back. She's used to young people coming down here for a few months then leaving to bigger and better things. She's bitter. Don't take it personally," Allen said.

"Andrew, Adam, Allen, and Allison, please report to the safari jeep zone for your silly reckless mission into the dark depths of the jungle. Also, we are out of Christmas ornaments in the gift shop. I repeat: We are out of Christmas ornaments in the gift shop," a voice over the loudspeaker said.

"Peculiar, it's only October," Allen said.

Allison stormed to Andrew and Adam's table and knocked a sandwich out of Andrew's hand as he was going to take a bite.

"Let's go, let's go. Meet me at the jeep in five minutes."

"Five minutes! Are we really going to have to ride with that pill?" Andrew muttered.

Andrew and Adam ran to their tent and threw together a sack full of supplies. Adam packed plenty of tank tops and mustache wax. Andrew made sure to bring the Jungle Navigation training manual which he hoped would guide him in the jungle. They met up with Dr. Marley, Allison, and Adam who were making final preparations by the jeep. Allison loaded her backpack onto the jeep and left for the artillery tent. Allen turned to Dr. Marley who was donning his lunch monocle.

"Sir, with all due respect, she's dangerous. She could get us killed out there, or worse, senselessly kill the animals," Allen said.

"Look, boys, Allison means well. Well, come to think of it, I don't think she actually *means* well. *But*, you're going to need her out there. She'll protect you more than you know. You have no idea what you could be up against in that temple. And by the end of this," he said as he removed his monocle, "you'll become closer than ever."

Allison returned carrying a trunk full of pistols, shotguns, and explosives.

"If you make it to the temple," Dr. Marley said as he placed his monocle on his left eye, "ammunition isn't going to do you any good."

Allison grunted and threw three guns out of the trunk to the ground. One misfired of into the jungle.

"Allison!" Dr. Marley screamed.

"What?! It didn't hit anybody!"

She placed the trunk into the jeep. Dr. Marley handed Allen the map. Allison took the wheel and Andrew and Adam hopped into the back. "Good lucks" were exchanged and as they were just beyond the trees, they could hear Dr. Marley shout.

"Don't forget about those apples!"

"What was that about *apples*?"Allen asked.

"Nothing, not worth explaining," Adam chuckled.

They drove through the afternoon along the river and then left the shore into the jungle. Allison warned them to be on high alert for game. They rejoined the river bed and decided that it was a cool enough place to take a break. They jumped out of the jeep and fueled up the car with one of their many jugs of gas. They also decided to cook some provisions over a fire. They were deep in the jungle, and on high alert. Andrew took out his Jungle Navigation Co. training manual and read the chapter about the annual summer talent show.

They gathered around the river as the food cooked over the fire. Allison looked over the map.

"Well, it looks like we've made good time. We've gone at least fifty miles at this point, and I think we've rejoined the river right here. We should be able to make camp this evening about half way to the Cambodian shrine," Allison said. The others nodded with approval—maybe she knew what she was doing after all.

They heard a rustle in the bushes.

"Get back to the jeep!" Allison screamed as she pulled out her trusty shotgun. She shot indiscriminately into the bushes.

"Stop it! Stop it," Allen shouted. "What are you doing? You have no reason to shoot."

"Fine." She took cover behind the jeep, "We can't be too sure. It could be a lion, or tiger or a bear."

"Oh, my!" Andrew said.

"There are no bears in Africa!" Allen shouted.

Andrew's nerves were shot. He made a break to the jeep and clung to a pistol he found in Allison's artillery trunk. Adam, completely unfazed, stood there twirling his mustache.

"Get back here!" Allen shouted.

The jungle fell silent for a few beats, then they heard a rustling again, now footsteps. Allen had taken cover behind the jeep, keeping a watchful eye on Allison. A few more rustles were heard, and more footsteps.

Dr. Marley casually walked out of the jungle brush, stunned to see the skippers.

"What in Sam Hill are you doing here? You've been gone for hours," he proclaimed.

"Well, you see—" Allison began.

"Look boys, you better get out there, stay along the river and do your job. The outpost is literally 500 meters *that* way."

Dr. Marley pushed back a branch that was covering a sign that read *Jungle Navigation Co. 500 Meters that way*. Right then, a Jungle Cruise steamer casually floated by full of tourists.

"Hi, folks!" Dr. Marley shouted.

"Who has been in charge of navigation? Doesn't matter. Andrew, take them to the temple. Follow the training book and you'll be fine." He removed his dinner monocle. "These old fools may be set in their ways, but you aren't."

"Aye, aye, sir."

"We're not on a boat, Andrew, you don't have to talk like that," Dr. Marley stated as he meandered farther into the jungle.

"You could have shot Dr. Marley; he is a saint around here!" Allen said, laying intoA llison. She mumbled and stumbled to compose a thought.

"*A saint!*" He screamed.

"Alright, you heard the man, lets get out of here and *actually* make our way towards the temple," Allen said.

Allison took a moment to recoup. She gazed at the river and took out her prized possession, a photo of her beloved *Allen*. They had arrived at the outpost at the same time; he had always been kind to her. She had taken a liking to him rather quickly. She loved his passion for animals. She loved his chiseled chin and bushy eyebrows. The photo brought her a calming sensation. Allen walked up behind her.

"Ready, Allison?"

Yes, my sweet beloved, she thought.

"Be right there," she grunted. She kissed the photo and put it in her left jacket pocket.

They packed up their gear. Adam elected to drive. Allen rode in the front with Andrew; Allison had been downgraded to the rear. Andrew instructed Adam to follow along the river for now. He continued to read the training book. He had honed in on the chapter about how to rescue passengers from the Cambodian temple. Allison snatched the training book.

"That book isn't going to do you any good now," she said as she threw it onto a rock in the river and chuckled to herself. Andrew crossed his arms in disgust and stared off into the river. They had traveled for many hours by that point.

"By my calculations we've been along the Amazon, the Congo, and have been traveling for niles and niles and niles. Let's set up camp up ahead before it gets too dark," Andrew stated.

They pulled up along the river and unpacked their med packs, food packs, and fanny packs. They took about a half hour to set up their tent. Allen chopped some fire wood. Allison stood by close to gaze at Allen while pretending to polish her shotgun.

Andrew and Adam sat along the river discussing their plan for the summer talent show. They had the juggling routine, the high-wire act, and the musical finale ready to go. Andrew noticed something floating down the river.

"What is that?"

"Looks like a bottle,"Adam responded. Adam was already shirtless so he took it upon himself to jump in the water and grab the bottle. Allen and Allison came to the river's edge to see what the commotion was all about.

"What is it?" Allen queried.

Adam came back to shore and popped the bottle open. A note fell out and he read it aloud. "S.O.S. A.S.A.P. B.Y.O.B. Send help! We are trapped in the Cambodian temple. Things are getting weird. Sincerely, Andrew." He stopped reading.

"It is dated four days from now," he said. Andrew was unnerved.

"Wh-wh-what? Lemme see that?" he said as he read it over. It *was* his handwriting. He had no recollection of writing it and it made absolutely no sense that it was written in the future. Allen was nervous.

"This isn't funny, Andrew. We are on a serious mission here, no need to play pranks," Allen said. It was no prank. Allison shook her head and went to the campfire.

Adam pocketed the letter and threw the bottle in the jeep and attempted to calm the crew. "Let's eat some food. Sound good. Andrew?"Adam was an excellent cook, and heated a skillet over the fire.

"Allison, would you like your filet mignon rare, medium, medium rare?" Adam asked.

"Well done," she responded.

"Well done?" Adam muttered, "what a waste."

Adam plated their meal, filet mignon with a peppercorn-crusted potato scallion. They gathered around the fire to eat.

"So, what's the craziest thing you've ever seen out here in the jungle?" Andrew asked the crew.

"I once saw a python luring in a gorilla with a banana," Allen said.

"One time with a tour we had settled in for the night along shore, and a school of barracudas attacked our boat. They jumped into the boat and started flipping and flapping all over the place. They managed to wrangle away our fishing poles, and then they floated off down the river. ... Luckily, our boat was empty at the time," Adam stated.

"Once, I was pulling away from the dock, and a few of my passengers refused to listen to me during my safety spiel," Allison said.

"Neat," Adam responded dryly.

"You know, I really appreciate you all coming out here and supporting me. I know in my heart those passengers are lost in that temple, and I think we have a pretty good tea...." Andrew began.

"Quiet," Allen interrupted, "do you hear that?"

"I do," Adam said.

"Sounds like five, no, four gorillas. Maybe they'll go away; put the fire out" Allen added.

Adam doused the fire out and hunkered down. The gorillas were getting closer. Allison took out her pistol and fired a few shots in the air. They were still coming.

"Get in the jeep," Allison said. They grabbed their backpacks and hopped into the jeep. Adam was at the helm. It wouldn't start.

"It won't turn over," Adam proclaimed.

"Let me try," Allison yelled as she shoved Adam out of the driver's seat. Nothing. The gorillas were mere meters away. Allison raced toward her trunk of guns and took them out with fervor.

"We need to leave on foot. We don't need to kill these gorillas. Lets go!" Allen shouted. Adam and Andrew obliged and fled into the jungle, Allison begrudgingly followed them. It was the dead of night, no moonlight reflecting on the river. Total darkness.

They stumbled onto what appeared to be a rocky cave next to a savannah. They decided to sleep there and figure out the next move at first morning light. Allison elected to take first watch to ensure no animals harmed them. Within moments, Andrew and Adam dozed off. While Allison cleaned her long gun, Allen took a seat next to her on a rock. Allen peered over to Allison.

"Thanks back there for being restrained with those gorillas. You could have easily shot into the jungle, and I noticed you...."

"I only had a few bullets left in my pistol, and my long guns were jamming. I wanted to save bullets in case they came," she responded.

"Oh, okay then," Allen replied with a smirk.

Allison was lying; she was carrying three other guns on her person at the time and could have easily shot more. She was taking to heart the things Allen was saying. She would never change for a man, but she was willing to make adjustments.

"Thanks to you, too. If you hadn't identified those gorillas, we could have been caught off guard more so than we already were," Allison said in a light tone.

"No problem at all. That's' my speciality."

"We seem to make a good team, you and I," Allison said with an inch of emotion.

"Maybe you're right," he said with a smile. Her heart melted in that moment. "I am going to get some sleep now. Wake me up in two hours and I will take over watch for you."

Allen fell asleep within minutes. Allison moved closer to Allen, right next to him, and stared at his beautiful chiseled chin. She built up the courage to put her arm around him as he slept. She felt at home, it was perfect. Allison dozed off seconds later.

A beautiful streak of purple and red filled the African sky. Birds chirped, water churned, and the wind blew a gentle breeze. It was sunrise, the most tranquil part of the day. The colors in the sky shifted from purple and red to blue and yellow, and the sun poked out from the horizon like a piece of shattered glass from a Jungle Cruise passenger's dropped bifocals. Andrew was not one to rise early, but this morning was different. The light of the sun peering over the horizon peacefully woke him up. He stretched and yawned.

He opened his eyes and shifted on his side to see the sun on the horizon. His eyes slowly focused and expanded his line of vision. He could see the nearby trees, the rocks, the river, and the animals. Hundreds and hundreds of animals gazing at him. He became wide eyed and slowly rolled over. *What were these animals doing and why were they looking at us?* His eyes adjusted again and he looked up to see a pride of lions protecting them while they slept. He nodded his head in approval and rolled over to snooze some more.

Wait, what? he thought as he became wide eyed, and quietly nudged Adam. "Shhhhhhhh," he whispered, "those lions are protecting us."

Adam woke up. Andrew crawled over to Allen and Allison, and nudged Allen awake.

"The lions are protecting us while we sleep," Andrew whispered.

"We need to leave right now," Allen whispered. The lions snarled, and panted heavily. Allen nudged Allison and whispered into her ear.

They quietly tip-toed away from the lions. Once they were about a dozen meters away, Allison screamed, "Run for your lives!"

They ran screaming and jumped into the river. They waded and swam out of pouncing range. They got out of the river and took rest on a bunch of rocks.

"Remind me to write you a 'thank you' card, Allison. You did a great job protecting us back there," Andrew yelled sarcastically.

"I-I don't know what happened. I was wide awake and then I was zonked out," Allison replied

"Ease it, Andrew," Adam cautioned.

"We could have been eaten alive, Adam! Why are you defending her?"

Adam grabbed Andrew by the ear and pulled him aside away from Allison and Allen, who were resting on a bed of rocks.

"Look, Andrew, us skippers have a bond out here. We drive out into the middle of the darkness of the jungle in a boat, into dangerous situations daily. We need support from one another. And it has to come from your heart. As soon as you prove yourself reliable to the bond of the skippers they won't be calling you 'rook,' and one day, if you're lucky, we may give you a nickname," Adam passionately proclaimed.

"Really?"

"Yeah, man. Well, when we sort this all out you'll be the hero of the outpost who saved everyone, so keep the possible vibes up, man, okay?"

"Okay, let's go to the temple," Andrew said. Andrew and Adam waded over to Allen and Allison.

"We are almost to Schweitzer Falls, so let's head there to refill our canteens," Andrew confidently proclaimed.

"That's a good plan, rook. There's also a stash of provisions and a dinghy there. We lost everything to those gorillas. We can replenish what we need before making the final trek to the Cambodian temple," Allen replied. They shared a knowing nod and walked along the shoreline to continue their journey.

"I had a nightmare last night, fellas. We were being chased by an elephant and a rhino and had to climb up a pole. What do you think it means?" Andrew asked.

"Eliphino," Allen quipped with a chuckle.

"Was Allen above or below me?" Allison asked. Allen gave her a puzzled.

"Was it a nightmare or was it premonition?" Adam wondered.

"Premonition? Wh-what's that?" Andrew asked.

"Nothing. Don't worry about it," Allen said. "Adam, this isn't one of your mystical stories, this is real life."

Adam twirled his handlebar mustache with a grin. He did that when he had touched another human's soul with a sense of doubt about the world order of things. He insisted it was part of his charm.

They walked for about an hour along the river. They heard the calming sounds of Schweitzer Falls. It was beautiful; a beacon of hope. It was the eighth wonder of the world. They jumped into the river and waded over to the falls. Allen declared he would grab the dinghy and provisions. Allison followed closely behind him. Adam and Andrew refilled their canteens and jugs with the fresh, clean water coming from the waterfall.

Adam filled his jug from the frontside as he had always done before. Andrew, however, did things a bit different. He went through the waterfall and filled his canteen with the backside of water.

"What are you doing?" Adam asked.

"Filling my jug."

Adam snatched Andrew's jug and dumped out the water. "You can't fill your canteen from the backside. Thats the most dangerous thing you can do."

"What do you mean?"

"What he means is complete nonsense. There are a few tall tales about the backside of water and how it is powerful and evil and all sorts of nonsense," Allen said.

"Say, Andrew, before that whole whirlpool opened up…. Had you stopped by Schweitzer Falls?" Adam asked.

"Y-yes."

"And when you did, did you fill up any canteens with water?"

"Yes."

"From the backside?"

"Yes."

"And what happened to those canteens just before the whirlpool opened up?" Adam asked.

"I-I-I don't remember."

"Welp, it looks like we are probably going to need the backside of water, so let's fill these canteens," Adam said as he filled up the canteen. He was a bit worried about what the future would hold.

Allison could be heard dragging a dinghy toward the water, nearby.

"Hey, everyone, the rook over here has been filling his canteens with the backside of water!" Allen proclaimed.

"I-I-I didn't know…" Andrew said nervously.

"Everyone knows that," Allison added.

"I don't believe in the stories, but I definitely don't play with *that* stuff," Allen said.

Andrew was full of shame. Allison came up to him and wrapped her arms around his shoulders.

"It's okay, rook, nobody's perfect. Now lets go rescue your passengers." Allen looked at Allison and smiled.

"You never told me that when I started, Allison," Adam said with a smirk.

Allen and Allison waded back to the dinghy along the shoreline. It had been commissioned in 1922 and named *Ol' Reliable*. It had seen better days. Today the wood was rotting and the hull was full of snakes. Allen did his best to remove the snakes safely, while Allison did her assessment of the dinghy.

"I think she's river worthy," she said unconfidently.

They hopped in and headed toward the temple. Allison and Adam took the first shift paddling down the river. There was a bit of rapids up ahead.

"Hold on, fellas!" Allison shouted.

Adam braced for the worst. Before they even reached the rapids, Adam's paddle broke. He proceeded to paddle with half a staff. Allison's paddle broke, too. She threw down the paddle and distributed life preservers to the others. A leak had now sprung. The dinghy took on water. It was slowly but surely sinking. Just before they reached the rapids, the dinghy had completely been engulfed with water.

"Link arms, we'll make it through this!" Allen yelled.

They bounced, jostled, and tussled through the rapids. It was getting worse. Up and down they bobbed in the water. They could see the end. Allison stroked to steer the crew away from the upcoming rocks, but it didn't work. She struck a rock clear to the head and was knocked unconscious. Allen cradled her head above water while Andrew and Adam stroked hard to get them to the shore. The water current was strong, but they prevailed. Allen carried Allison out and plopped her onto the ground.

"She's not breathing!"

"CPR hasn't been invented yet!" Adam shouted.

"You have to save her, Andrew!" Allen screamed.

"Why do I have to be the one?"

"'Cause it would be weird if I did!"

"Why?"

"'Cause I like her!"

"You like her?" Adam asked with a smile.

Andrew reluctantly breathed into her mouth. She wasn't responding. Andrew rolled her on her side and slapped her back. Allison coughed up a ton of water and took a deep breath. She had recovered.

"You saved me."

"Of course," Andrew replied.

"You should rest a moment," Allen said as he helped her sit up on a rock.

"Thanks, Andrew. Thanks for everything." Andrew knowingly nodded and handed her a canteen of water.

"I just swallowed a ton of water. Why would you hand me this?"

Allen stood aside. He had admitted his feelings toward Allison in the heat of the moment. *Had she heard*? he thought as he gazed at her longingly.

"You okay, Allen?" Adam asked.

"Yes, yes, I'm fine. Just was concerned with Allison here."

They regained their composure and walked along the river. Allen helped Allison, who hobbled, and at this point was milking it, just to be close to Allen. They were approaching familiar territory and knew they were getting close. They passed around the river bend and saw a sign *100 meters to the Cambodian Temple.*

"There it is," Adam proclaimed.

"Thanks, Captain Obvious," Allison quipped.

72 Hours Earlier

Andrew navigated his Jungle Cruise boat toward the Cambodian temple. The boat was full of tourists who were in awe of the ruins around them.

"Up ahead you'll see the Cambodian temple. It looks like there was an earthquake here, nothing to be *shook up* about," he said as he pointed to a few of the collapsed beams that once stood. He had navigated this route before. This time he had an idea. There had been a little boy at the front named Billy asking him all sorts of questions about the jungle. He felt a connection to him and wanted to inspire the next generation of skippers.

"Hey, little Billy, would you want to take over the helm, and drive us through the temple? You could be my first mate," Andrew asked.

"Gee, that would be swell!" Little Billy said.

Billy's eyes grew wide and he had a grin larger than the Mekong River. Andrew motioned for little Billy to take the helm. Andrew was right behind him with one hand help him steer.

"This is the best day of my life!" Little Billy said.

Andrew was feeling really good about himself and decided to take a sip out of his trusty canteen. Just then, a Bengal tiger roared, scaring the child back and knocking him into Andrew. Andrew lost his footing, and dropped the canteen into the water. Andrew thought nothing of it for a moment. Things became darker and darker in the temple, more so than usual.

The boat slowed down and Andrew revved up the engine. *What's going on?* he thought. The current of the river flowed backwards and there was a strong breeze coming from in front of them. The boat moved backwards slowly. The passengers grew a bit weary.

"Nothing to worry about, folks! The propeller must be stuck in some mud. We'll be back on our way sho..."

"*AHHHH!!!!*" a woman screamed from behind the boat. "Look!"

She pointed toward the waters behind a storm that had brewed inside the temple, and a whirlpool that had formed, sucking in water all around. The current flowed faster. Andrew throttled up the engine to *Kwango Kate* as much as he could, but she simply couldn't handle it. The engine gave off a loud explosion. The passengers screamed. The engine had internally combusted. The lights on the boat were extinguished and the radio was dead. The boat swirled in a circle, rushing in the whirlpool. Then the whirlpool transformed into a vortex, water in the center disappearing below.

They swirled lower and lower.

"Put on your life jackets, and no flash photography, please!" Andrew screamed.

Andrew raced through the boat toward the life-jacket crate. As he did, he slapped a passenger's camera out of their hands as they were attempting to take a flash picture.

"I said *no* flash pictures!" Andrew screamed.

He made it to the crate and burst it open with the emergency crow bar. He found nothing inside.

"Where are they?!" Andrew screamed.

Little Billy had followed him. "Look!" He pointed to a piece of paper while all hell was breaking loose around them. Andrew snatched it and read the little note.

"I.O.U one crate of life jackets—Sincerely, T.K.," Andrew read.

"Damnit, Trevor!" he shouted toward the heavens with a fist shake. "Everyone hold on to something that will float!"

The boat continued to swirl to its doom. Andrew made his way back to the helm.

"Does this mean the meal service is cancelled?" a passenger asked.

"Yes!"

"Can I order one last drink before we land?" another passenger queried.

"No!"

"Will there still be a...."

"Never mind!" Andrew screamed as he ran faster, navigating the luggage that had been strewn about.

"Hold on, everyone!" he yelled as they got lower toward the vortex center.

"This sure is taking a long time!" a passenger shouted.

"Almost there!" Andrew replied.

Andrew woke up in what could be described only as a massive cavern in the temple. There were hundreds of ancient statues strewn about with gold-plated accents shimmering from the light of a nearby fire. It was the *Kwango Kate*. She had split in two and her engine was ablaze in flames. A waterfall flowed down the center of the room and a stream of water ran out through a small hole in the rocks.

Andrew looked around and saw his passengers scattered about the various rocks in the cavern. He went to everyone's aid and ensured they were all okay. They were shaken up, but they managed to have only a few scratches. Even Little Billy was in positive spirits. Andrew gathered all the passengers and assembled them next to the remains of the burning *Kwango Kate*.

"Everyone is going to be fine, we just need to find a way out. Let's gather supplies while there is still something left on the boat. That waterfall should provide us plenty of fresh water to drink," Andrew said.

"Who put you in charge?!" Thomas Galvindale, a passenger, shrieked.

"*SHUT UP, DAD!*" Little Billy Galvindale replied, with a hard swat at his father's ear.

"I'm the captain of this boat, and I will keep you all safe. This type of thing happens all the time," Andrew said.

It didn't, but that kind of statement calmed the passengers. He motioned for a few of them to help him douse the fire out on the boat. They put it out quickly.

They examined the area. The walls were all closed in, and there was an underground river, but that would be far too dangerous to navigate.

"We need to move rocks and tunnel our way out. That stream flowing through the rocks over there, it has to lead somewhere. We will work in shifts. Let's get moving," Andrew said.

"Do you have any kind of dynamite? Could we just blow the whole thing up?" Thomas Galvindale asked.

"*SHUT UP, DAD!*" Little Billy screamed.

"No, no, Little Billy, that's not a bad idea. Unfortunately, we don't have any. For safety reasons, we don't carry that kind of stuff on our boats."

"Don't be stupid, Dad," Billy said.

The passengers divided up. One set began to organize their possessions, and the others dug up rocks above the stream. They piled them quickly to create a tunnel. The waterfall flowed more and more, causing the water level to rise.

"We're going to have to move quickly or this whole place could flood," Andrew said to the passengers working the first shift.

Several hours went by. In fact, it was already the next day. It was tricky keeping track of time in a cave. Especially *this* cave. They managed to keep a fire going and had enough provisions to last a long time. Their main concern was the fast flow of water that kept the water level rising.

They were about three shifts in, and the cavern was almost completely flooded. There was too much water, and it didn't have enough room to flow. They moved their provisions to higher ground, but the flooding waters kept rising. They moved rocks almost completely engulfed in water.

"We've got to do something else! We're going to drown!" Thomas yelled.

"*SHUT UP, DAD!*" Little Billy screamed from the top of an ancient sacred monkey statue.

"Get off that brass monkey, Billy! It's all funky," Thomas replied. It was covered in a green slime.

Right then, Andrew was banging away at rocks in the bottom of the hole. He punctured something that caused hundreds of rocks to fall forward. They had found a way out! The water flowed downward and everyone gathered by the tunnel to see what lay ahead. They managed to create make-shift torches with the mangled supplies.

They followed through and reached a grand atrium. There were six different streams flowing through tunnels, all leading in different directions. Above each tunnel, there was a large silver animal statue including a tiger, an elephant, and even a hippopotamus. The waters were flowing fast. *Maybe this is our chance to get help,* Andrew thought. They were in the heart of the temple.

"I need pencil, paper, and bottles with corks. Everyone look in your bags," Andrew said.

Little Billy ran back to grab bottles, and a few passengers supplied a pencil and some paper scraps. He wrote down several notes and dated them.

"This could help the outpost know where we are," Andrew said, much to the delight of the passengers. He placed each bottle in a different stream and they swiftly were off.

"You don't actually think anyone would ever find one of those things, do you?" Thomas grumpily said.

"*SHUT UP, DAD!*" Little Billy shouted as he slapped his dad's arm.

"No, I will not 'shut up'!" Thomas screamed.

"I'm tired of taking orders from this kid! He's basically a child and he is not responsible enough to get us to safety," Thomas added.

"He's gotten us this far," a passenger said.

"Well, it's not far enough. He'd like us to simply wait here for someone to rescue us...."

"I never said tha...." Andrew interrupted.

"Enough! I am tired of being told what to do," Thomas said. Andrew was a bit shaken up.

"Sir, please calm down, there are children here."

"I will not *calm down*," Thomas yelled as he shoved Andrew to the ground.

Andrew bumped his head on a rock and rolled into the stream. A passenger jumped in to help him, but it was too late. Andrew had washed down the river toward the elephant statue.

"You've killed him!" the passenger said as he got out of the water. He raced toward Thomas to tackle him, and Thomas quickly pulled out a revolver.

"Now, everyone cool it!"

"Where did you get that?" the passenger asked.

"What are you doing, Dad?" Little Billy added.

"It's for emergency situations only, and this is an emergency!" Thomas said.

The passenger stopped in his tracks.

"I am taking my destiny into my own hands. I don't care what happens to all of you, but right before we went into this hell I saw a tiger. Therefore, I am going to head down the stream under the tiger statue. Who's with me!?" Thomas said.

He grabbed Little Billy by the arm, and a few passengers begrudgingly went with him. He took the first leap into the water and swam toward the Tiger with Billy in his hands.

"*No, Dad!*" Billy screamed.

The passengers followed right behind and the river flowed faster and faster.

"*Nooo!* What have I done?!" Thomas' words echoed through the temple, "I immediately regret this!"

The screams subsided, and six passengers were left there pondering what to do next.

Present

Andrew, Adam, Allen, and Allison were standing at the foot of the temple beside the water. Allison grabbed a few pieces of wood to help them float along into the temple.

"Let's do this," Allen said as he plopped into the river. They all followed behind holding onto the drift wood and their backpacks.

"So it's come to this!" Adam said.

"I can't believe we finally made it!" Andrew screamed.

There was a bit of excitement in the group. They floated quite a ways and found a nook to get out and rest up on shore.

"I don't see the boat anywhere," Allison said with frustration.

"Now, Andrew, what specifically happened, that day," Allen asked.

"It's all so fuzzy. I remember a whirlpool, I remember a kid named Billy, a tig...."

"A tiger?! What happened with the tiger?" Adam asked.

"Well, let me think, we were just entering the temple, and then the tiger roared and Little Billy knocked into me, which knocked my canteen into the water," Andrew replied.

"You mean the canteen full of the backside of water?" Adam asked.

"Yes!" Andrew said as he was reaching for his canteen. He jumped into the water and swam toward the entrance.

"You're going to want to brace yourself for this. Grab hold of something that floats!" Andrew yelled.

Allison grabbed hold of Allen.

"Allison?"

"Yes, Allen?"

"You're standing on my foot." He said.

Andrew had almost made his way to the throat of the temple. He screwed off the top of his canteen filled with the backside of water and dumped it. Allison, Allen, and Adam were close behind him and watched him pour it in. Nothing happened.

"I knew this was a complete waste of time!" Allison yelled.

"Cool it, Allison," Allen said as he gave her a gentle caress on her cheek in the water. It hasn't been a complete waste; at least we got to be together."

Allen grabbed hold of Allison and gave her a big kiss on the lips.

Adam and Andrew were close to one another and exchanged shocked looks. Allison and Allen went toward the shoreline in the temple and kissed more and more.

"Oh, Allen!" Allison said.

"I'd give anything for this to stop," Andrew muttered toward Adam in the water.

The temple rumbled. The wind howled and the waters began to spin in a circle.

"That'll work! Here we go," Andrew proclaimed. The torrent of the whirlpool spun faster and faster, and the water level rose, pulling in Allison and Allen who were still embraced.

"I love you, Allen!" Allison yelled as she clung to him as they went down.

"Ooh, love? That's...a bit strong. Can we take things slow?"

The waters flowed faster and faster, circling around toward the vortex. Eventually, they were engulfed in a water flush that felt like it went on for weeks.

They fell one last time, down into a pool of water, into the same cavern Andrew had inhabited before. Andrew and Adam washed up on the rocks and Allen pulled up Allison to safety. They were in complete darkness and heard voices.

"Hello!?" Andrew yelled throughout the cavern.

Voices could be heard and light appeared from a tunnel.

"It's Andrew!" someone yelled.

"Huh?" Allison said.

The voices and the light grew. It was the passengers Andrew had left behind!

"Andrew, we were so worried! When you fell into the river toward the elephant statue, Thomas fled and a few others jumped in the stream toward the tiger statue just a few minutes ago," a passenger said.

"Wait, what? When did I fall in the river toward an "elephant statue"?"

"It couldn't have been more than three minutes ago," the passenger said.

Adam's eyes lit up. Something was strange in this temple, time traveled differently.

"I've been with my friends here for the past couple of days...." Andrew said.

Other passengers chimed in and assured him that it had just happened a moment ago. They filled him in on what had happened. He was declared a hero. He was reminded of that horrid Thomas Gavlindale. Pieces of the puzzle were starting to form, but it felt like a distant memory that he had never really had.

"We need to follow Thomas. He could be in trouble," Andrew said.

"Lead the way," Allison said with a gleam in her eye.

They raced toward the six streams. It was all there just as the passengers had told him a moment ago. Adam took notice of a bottle wedged on a rock near a stream.

"What's this?" Adam asked. He picked it up, uncorked it, and took a look at the paper inside.

"Just about ten minutes ago Andrew sent bottles in different directions," a passenger said.

"It worked, we got one of the messages.... About a day and a half ago."

"That makes no sense," Allen said. Adam tossed him the bottle.

"Look's like we're beyond sense now, man," Adam replied.

Andrew took a look at the writing on the note and remembered writing it. It just felt like it was a distant memory, not something that had happened ten minutes ago.

Andrew dropped the bottle and it shattered into a hundred pieces.

"Thomas and the other passengers went that way?" Andrew asked as he pointed toward the stream that went underneath the tiger statue.

"Yup," a passenger replied.

"And they screamed mercilessly wishing they hadn't done it."

"Yup!"

"Well, what are we waiting for?!" Andrew hopped in the water and the others followed suit. They swam with him and they all locked arms.

"If we stick together, we should be all right," he added. The waters raced faster and faster. The torrents sucked a few of them under the water, but they held tight. They heard screams in the distance.

"*Save us!*"

The screams were growing louder and louder. The water began to flow *upstream* toward the rooftop of the cavern. A tornado of water was flowing upward with Thomas, Little Billy, and the other passengers. At the top of the tornado of water a Bengal tiger spirit was formed in the water. It was laughing.

"What do we do?!" Andrew shouted.

"You come here seeking the secrets of the after life?!" the Bengal tiger spirit spoke.

"*NO!* None of us want that!" Andrew shouted.

"Well, I might be interested in that," Thomas said, swirling in the opposite direction of Andrew.

"*SHUT UP, DAD!*" Little Billy screamed. He managed to swim toward Andrew, leaving his dad smiling on his own.

"You seek things beyond your comprehension!" the tiger bellowed throughout the tornado.

"No! None of us seek anything but the way out of here!" Allen screamed.

"Are you sure?!" the Tiger replied.

"Yes!" Adam added.

"This doesn't make sense, this is supposed to say to be a peaceful temple," Allen screamed toward his fellow Skippers.

"Enough of this!" Allison shrieked. She managed to reach into her backpack and take out a few pistols. She threw them to Adam and Andrew who fumbled them in their hands.

"Shoot!" She screamed.

"Where?!"

"Toward the iger!"

They obliged and shot upwards toward the Bengal tiger spirit. This made him angry.

"You will now see horrible things beyond your imagination!" the tiger screamed. The vortex raced upwards. Thomas screamed and was sucked into the mouth of the Bengal tiger spirit.

"Dad!" Little Billy screamed. "We've got to save him."

"It's okay, we're all going to die some time. Probably really soon," Allison said in a comforting voice.

"I've got it!" Adam screamed. "Andrew, hand me one of your canteens!"

Andrew threw one of his canteens toward Adam.

"We've got to dump it in!" Adam yelled as he swirled closer and closer toward the top.

"You're right! The polarization must be off from good and evil, the ying and the yang!" Allen yelled.

Adam unscrewed the cap and dumped it into the vortex. Nothing happened.

"Well, I'm all out of ideas," Adam stated.

"Hey, rook, was that one of the canteens with the backside of water?!" Allison shouted from several meters away.

"Well, yes," Andrew said.

"Come on, rook!" she shouted.

Everyone muttered in disappointment. The tiger laughed maniacally as his victims rose closer and closer.

"We need the *frontside* of water to reverse the balance!" Allen yelled.

Andrew frantically reached into his backpack and found another canteen. This one was properly labeled *Frontside of Water.*

"Dump it!" everyone screamed.

The water poured upwards into the vortex and a warm peaceful glow emerged. It radiated toward the Bengal tiger spirit. The spirit roared throughout the vortex that began to slow down.

"It's working! You did it, Andrew!" Allison yelled.

As the water slowed, the spirit tiger transformed into a cyclone in front of their eyes. It burst through the ceiling of the cavern and rose toward the heavens. The passengers and crew were blasted out, landing hundreds of meters away safely. Even Thomas and Little Billy made it unscathed.

"You don't see something like that everyday," Adam said, "But I do."

Everyone groaned.

They gathered their composure and made their way toward the river they could hear off in the distance. Along the way, they stumbled upon a middle-aged man. He appeared to be knocked out. Allen raced toward him to wake him.

"He has a pulse!" Allen said.

He banged on his back causing a bit of water to fall out. The man coughed.

"He's alive!" Allen shouted, "Sir, are you okay?"

"Yes, yes, where am I?"

"You're in the middle of the jungle," Andrew said.

'Oh, right, right, right. I was in the jungle, and then I fell in the water and then into the temple. Then you wouldn't believe what happened."

"Try us!" Andrew said. Everyone laughed.

"What's your name, anyway?" Adam asked.

"Timothy. I'm with the Jungle Navigation Co."

"Timothy? By any chance, were you out here looking for apples?" Adam asked.

"Apples?" Allen questioned in a confused manner.

"Why, yes, yes, I was. How did you know?" Timothy said.

"Just a hunch," Adam replied.

It looked like they had found Dr. Marley's long-lost friend. He was tattered and confused, of course, but it seemed like something had happened in that temple. And whatever had happened to Timothy, had been undone by Andrew.

"Let's go home," Andrew said triumphantly, lending a hand to Timothy. Everyone, feeling relieved, continued on the river. They approached the waters and saw hundreds of elephants bathing.

"It's okay to take pictures, folks," Andrew said."They've got their trunks on."

"We almost just died," Thomas said.

Dr. Marley stood nervously along the edge of the dock. He had got the word that the missing passengers and heroic crew had been picked up by *Congo Connie* a few hours ago and were almost back. He had lined up several skippers on the dock who had fresh blankets and clothes.

Congo Connie came around the bend and everyone cheered.

"Ahoy!" Dr. Marley shouted.

The boat pulled up to the dock and the passengers were unloaded in an orderly fashion. The passengers shook hands with the skippers who gave them a hearty welcome. Hugs and high-fives were also given to Andrew, Adam, Allison, and Allen who brought up the rear.

"Timothy! Is that really you?" Dr. Marley gave him a big hug. "Wow." He looked at him up and down, and removed his dock monocle." Time has ravaged your once youthful looks."

Timothy gave him a backslap, as Dr. Marley addressed the crowd.

"We want to thank you from the bottom of our heart for trusting us with your business. We'd like to extend you a 10% discount on your next Jungle Cruise tour! Not only that, but a 5% discount at the gift shop," he said while motioning toward it.

All was right at the Jungle Navigation Co. ... for now.

The Real Housewives of the Haunted Mansion

a Liberty Square play in one act by Kristen Waldbieser

Cast of Characters

Madame Carlotta St. Demark: A spirit celebrating her 71st Death Day. She is over-the-top, extravagant, and speaks with a loud Southern accent. She is always the center of attention.

Lucretia Bluebeard: Carlotta's party planner. She is beautiful, but often overlooked. She is usually annoyed, except when near the unrequited love of her life, Pickwick.

Constance Hatchaway: The Merry Murderess of the Haunted Mansion, a title given to her after killing all three of her husbands. Everyone is terrified of her, which she loves.

Madame Leota: Responsible for summoning spirits to the mansion, the maternal figure of everyone. She speaks only in rhyme and insists others do as well.

Erasmus Cromwell Pickwick: The life of the party. Hopelessly in love with Carlotta, and often blinded to others around him because of it.

Harriet von Clair: A famous opera singer in her former life. She is the definition of a diva, but still very kind. She will ensure that no one steals her spotlight.

Fiancé: Constance's new fiancé. A man of few words.

Ensemble: Ensemble members will play various roles such as decorators, chefs, and mansion residents.

Scene

Gracey Manor, otherwise known as the Haunted Mansion

TIME: 1904

Scene 1

SETTING: We are in the grand ballroom of GRACEY MANOR, a beautiful gothic mansion that has since been haunted by 999 Happy Haunts. In the center of the room, there is a long table with a grand cake at the head seat. In the room, you see a grand organ, as well as an ornate chandelier hanging from the ceiling.

AT RISE: The entire CAST is frozen on stage, in various places throughout the room. CARLOTTA is standing at the edge of a long table, about to blow out the candles on the grand cake. LUCRETIA and HARRIET are seated at the table next to her. CONSTANCE dances with her FIANCÉ, among a large group of WALTZING DEAD. PICKWICK hangs from the large chandelier above. As they turn to the audience to speak, a spotlight shines on them, with the rest of the lights dim.

PICKWICK
(to audience)

Welcome, foolish mortals, to
the Haunted Mansion.

CARLOTTA
(to audience)

I am your host. Your ghost host.

LUCRETIA
(to audience)

Our story begins here, in this ballroom.
Here you will see happy haunts mate-
rializing for a swinging gathering.

(The lights begin to rise, revealing
the rest of the scene behind them. The
cast begins to move in slow motion.)

CONSTANCE
(to audience)

There's no turning back now.

HARRIET
(to audience)

We invite you to listen to the tale of
dear Carlotta. A story that has become
one of our favorites here in the mansion.

(At the mention of her name, CARLOTTA
tries to blow out the candles on her
cake, the spotlight on her intensifying.)

MADAME LEOTA
(to audience)

Every ghost and ghoul has a different
tale from this night. They all have their
own way of explaining our delight.

ALL
(to audience)

Of course, there's always *my* way.

(BLACKOUT)

(END OF SCENE)

Scene 2

SETTING: In the ballroom, earlier that day.

AT RISE: CARLOTTA is the only one on
stage. SHE walks around the room,
inspecting every detail. SHE steps in
front of a large mirror, and twirls in
front of it, clearly pleased with her
appearance. SHE moves center, and looks
directly at the audience. SHE smiles.

CARLOTTA
(to audience)

It was simply goin' to be a night that
would be remembered foreva'. Ah, yes, the
night of my 71st Death Day Celebration!
    Oh, for you corruptible mortals,
instead of celebratin' our birthdays,
we here celebrate our Death Days, the
day we arrived at this precious little
mansion. Granted, most only celebrate
their 5th or 20th or what-not, but let's
face it. Every year that I live in the
mansion, it's a gift to all. So why
shouldn't I get a few gifts in return?

(She giggles.)

Now, I had everythin' perfectly in place.
I had attended to every little detail.
Made sure everythin' was the way I wanted
it to be. It would be the biggest soiree

ya'll have ever seen! Because frankly,
my dears, that's just what I deserved.

(DECORATORS and CHEFS run in to the
room, carrying large decorations, food
choices, and party supplies, all in
beautiful colors of rose gold and pink.
THEY are very frantic, very nervous.)

CARLOTTA
(to audience)

Well, it's about time.

(CARLOTTA turns away from the audience
and joins the scene. SHE walks over to
DECORATOR 1, who is carrying a large
bouquet of pink roses. CARLOTTA shakes her
head, annoyed. SHE approaches DECORATOR
2, who is carrying a gold banner for the
wall, at which CARLOTTA rolls her eyes.
Finally, SHE tastes the food that the CHEF
has brought in, and spits it right out.)

CARLOTTA

No, no! It's just not right! The decor
needs to be grander! The food needs to
be somethin' special and different! This
is not some li'l mad tea party ya'll are
throwin'! It needs to be bigger! Bigger!

DECORATOR 1

But, Carlotta…

CARLOTTA

Excuse me, was I finished?

DECORATOR 1

Oh, it sounded like you were.

CARLOTTA

Excuse me! No! I want all of this gone!
You'd think this was a darlin' little
baby's first birthday, for Pete's sake!

DECORATOR 1

Well, we were going for...

CARLOTTA

This party needs to materialize into
somethin' marvelous quick. Not somethin' ghostly. I mean, ghastly. Well,
it should be ghostly, but not ghastly.
Because the last thing anyone wants is
a ghastly, ghostly party. Are we clear?

(DECORATOR 1 pauses to think.)

CARLOTTA

Are we clear?!

DECORATOR 1

Yes! Of course, Carlotta. We
just thought the rose and the
gold really complimented...

CARLOTTA

Lovely chattin' with you, suga'.
I'll see you at the party!

(CARLOTTA twirls away from DECORATOR 1
and waves behind her, leaving them to
figure out exactly what it was that she
said. CARLOTTA turns to the audience.)

CARLOTTA
(to audience)

I felt that I was perfectly clear.
Certainly, I wasn't askin' too much.
I deserved the social gatherin' of
the century. Did they simply not
understand that? Surely, they'd get
it right eventually. Even if they
needed a little more guidance.

(CARLOTTA continues to inspect the
room. DECORATORS 1 & 2 have moved
downstage left, whispering to avoid
being heard by their hostess.)

DECORATOR 2

What does she think of the decorations?

DECORATOR 1

Ghastly.

DECORATOR 2

Ghastly?

DECORATOR 1

No, ghostly.

DECORATOR 2

They're ghostly?

DECORATOR 1

No, she wanted them to be ghostly,
not ghastly. The party can not be
ghastly, but it should be ghostly.

(They pause.)

To be honest, I'm really not sure
how I remembered all that.

(CARLOTTA squeals as the CHEF enters,
carrying a massive cake covered
in black and purple roses.)

CARLOTTA

Oh, finally! One of you darlins'
finally did somethin' right!

(The DECORATORS roll their eyes.)

CARLOTTA

It's gorgeous! To die for! Now, skedaddle! Shoo! My guests will be arrivin' any
minute, and you must have everythin' done!

(CARLOTTA pushes everyone out of the ballroom, and THEY are clearly happy to go.
CARLOTTA turns back to the audience.)

CARLOTTA
(to audience)

I've ensured that only the best spirits
would be invited. No little hooligans, no hitchhikers, would be causin'
any sort of shenanigans on my special
night. The very thought of it! Not to
worry, though. My dear sweet friend,
Lucretia, bless her heart, was takin'
care of all that. She's such a doll,
volunteerin' to help plan my party!

(SHE turns back to the ballroom)

Lucretia!

(LUCRETIA is not quick to enter the
room. She enters slowly, carrying a
clipboard with a large stack of papers

on top, the notes that Carlotta has
given her for the party. She smiles
sweetly, but it is clearly fake.)

                LUCRETIA

            Yes, Carlotta?

                CARLOTTA

        Sweet pea, I'm sure you've
          been hard at work!

                LUCRETIA

        You guessed it, Carlotta.

                CARLOTTA

        I trust all the table assign-
        ments have been made correctly?

                LUCRETIA

          Of course, Carlotta.

                CARLOTTA

    And the music. An endless waltz shall
    be played all evening, is that true?

                LUCRETIA

          Absolutely, Carlotta.

                CARLOTTA

    And only those on the guest list
        have been invited, true?

                LUCRETIA

        That's really the definition of
          a guest list, Carlotta.

CARLOTTA

Well, then! You've got work
to do! Hop to it!

(LUCRETIA turns away, rolling her
eyes as she walks offstage left.
CARLOTTA turns to the audience.)

CARLOTTA

Everythin' was goin' to be perfect. Every
detail, every decision, I made sure it
was flawless. As the most beloved spirit
in this delightful mansion, everyone
wanted it to be a night talked about
forever! Oh, they all just adore me!

(BLACKOUT)

(END OF SCENE)

Scene 3

SETTING: The library. Books are stacked
from floor to ceiling, and marble busts of
the greatest ghost writers the literary
world has ever known line the shelves.

AT RISE: LUCRETIA stands alone, center
stage, holding a stack of invitations, twice the size of her.

LUCRETIA
(to audience)

Dear mortals, there are a few things
that you have the right to know. First
of all, I can't stand Carlotta. Oh, I'm
sure you're not wondering why. You've now
spent six minutes with her, and I'm sure
you're feeling the same way. The second
thing you should know, she's not Southern.

She's from Rhode Island. So all the little "sweet peas" and "darlins'" are straight from her made up Southern belle backstory. The last thing you should know? I plan on making this party a complete disaster.

(HARRIET and PICKWICK enter stage right, laughing and talking indistinctly. LUCRETIA sees them, and while balancing the stack of invitations, fixes her dress and hair.)

LUCRETIA
(to audience)

And he's why.

(LUCRETIA approaches HARRIET and PICKWICK.)

LUCRETIA

Hello, Pickwick.

PICKWICK

Oh, hello, um…

HARRIET

Hello, dear, Lucretia! What brings you here today?

LUCRETIA

Oh, right.

(SHE clears her throat and reads.)

"The Grand Carlotta humbly requests your presents at the 71st Anniversary of her Death Day."

(SHE tosses HARRIET her invitation. SHE kindly passes PICKWICK his invitation, who opens it quickly.)

PICKWICK

Did you say Carlotta? *The* Carlotta?!
I've heard so many stories about
her, so many wonderful things. This
is such an incredible honor!

LUCRETIA

Clearly you've never met her.

PICKWICK

I've always wanted to. But, just what do
you say to such a marvelous ghoul? No,
unfortunately, our paths have yet to cross.

LUCRETIA
(to herself)

Lucky you.

HARRIET

Tell Carlotta that we wouldn't miss
it for the underworld. Oh, her 23rd
Death Day party was just to die for.

LUCRETIA

Well, trust me, you won't want to
miss this one. I guarantee it.

PICKWICK

I wouldn't dream of it! Just to be
invited! She thought to invite me!
I'm just speechless, really I am.

LUCRETIA

I'll be there as well, Pickwick.

PICKWICK   LUCRETIA
(at the same time) (at the same time)

Perhaps Carlotta will Perhaps we could
share share a dance with me! a dance?

PICKWICK

How many were invited?

LUCRETIA

Oh. 997.

PICKWICK

And I made the list!

LUCRETIA

Congratulations, what an accomplishment.

PICKWICK

But...what should I get her? It
has to be the perfect gift!

HARRIET

Good question. What do you get
the ghoul who has everything?

(LUCRETIA smiles. She sees a piece
of her plan coming into play.)

LUCRETIA

You know, Harriet, Carlotta is
such a big fan of your music.

HARRIET

She is? A fan of mine?

LUCRETIA
(laying it on thick)

Absolutely! Oh, I can't tell you how many
times she's told me that she admires your
talents so much. You know what? A performance at her party would just mean
the world to her, I'm sure of it! I mean,
who wouldn't want the great Harriet
von Clair to perform at their party?

HARRIET

You're absolutely right! Who wouldn't
want me to perform at their party?

LUCRETIA

Literally what I just said.

HARRIET

I'll do it!

LUCRETIA

Wonderful!

PICKWICK

I just can't believe it. I'm
going to Carlotta's party!

LUCRETIA

I'll see you there, Pickwick.

PICKWICK

Of course! I wouldn't miss
my dear Carlotta's day!

LUCRETIA

Right.

(PICKWICK and HARRIET exit, discussing what PICKWICK should get for Carlotta's gift. LUCRETIA turns back to the audience.)

LUCRETIA
(to audience)

I know, he might not be the sharpest shovel in the graveyard. But the fact of the matter is, his obsession with Carlotta needs to end. And once he sees, once they all see, who Carlotta really is, he'll realize I've been here all along.

(BLACKOUT)

(END OF SCENE)

Scene 4

SETTING: The grand ballroom. It has now been decorated to fit Carlotta's standards, adorned in beautiful black and purple. A haunting waltz is being played on a grand organ.

AT RISE: The ballroom is filled with PARTY GUESTS, eagerly awaiting their hostess' arrival. HARRIET, PICKWICK, and PARTY GUEST 1 stand downstage right.

HARRIET

Shouldn't she be arriving soon? It is her party after all.

PARTY GUEST 1

Oh, you know, all the best
ghouls are fashionably late.

PICKWICK

I just can't wait to see her!

(LUCRETIA enters through the large
doors center stage, but no one seems to
notice. SHE spots PICKWICK, takes a deep
breath, and approaches the group.)

LUCRETIA

Hello, Pickwick.

PICKWICK

Oh, Lilianna.

LUCRETIA

It's Lucretia.

PICKWICK

Right. Lucinda.

LUCRETIA

Right. Um, earlier you had mentioned dancing…

PICKWICK

I certainly did! Oh, I love to dance!

(HE twirls LUCRETIA around and around,
and SHE giggles. It is the first time
you see her genuinely smile.)

LUCRETIA

Do you think, perhaps, that when
it comes time for a waltz…

PICKWICK

Do you think Carlotta will dance with me?

LUCRETIA

Oh, I don't know. She really hates dancing.

PICKWICK

Well, she's never danced with me.

(HE dips LUCRETIA, holding her.)

LUCRETIA

Right.

(She sighs.)

I'm sure she would be delighted.

(The lights go down, and a lavish
fanfare starts to play. The entire
cast is hushed. A spotlight shines on
the door center stage. The doors are
thrown open, and CARLOTTA stands, striking an over-the-top pose. PICKWICK
drops LUCRETIA to the ground.)

CARLOTTA

Darlins'! How delighted I am
to see all of ya'll!

(CARLOTTA parades around the room,
blowing kisses and waving to all of her
guests, who are applauding her entrance.
LUCRETIA stares blankly at the audience.)

                          LUCRETIA
                        (to audience)

        Well, no one can say that she doesn't
            know how to make an entrance.

(CARLOTTA crosses downstage right, waiting
for her guests to approach her, and they
quickly do. PICKWICK pushes past LUCRETIA,
causing her to fall on the chair behind
her. PICKWICK runs over to CARLOTTA, followed by HARRIET and other PARTY GUESTS.)

                          PICKWICK

        Oh, Carlotta! Do open my gifts first!

                          HARRIET

            No, I have such a gift for you!
            Do let me give it to you first!

                          CARLOTTA

            Sweeties, you shouldn't have
        brought me any gifts! Your pres-
        ence is, well, present enough!

                  (She snaps her fingers.)

                          Lucretia!

(LUCRETIA takes her time walking over to
CARLOTTA, taking an especially long time
as she passes PICKWICK. You can see the
agitation in CARLOTTA'S face growing.)

                          CARLOTTA

            Lucretia! Be a doll and take
        these over to the gift table.

                          LUCRETIA

                     With pleasure.

(LUCRETIA takes the stack of gifts
from PICKWICK and the other GUESTS.
She walks them over to the other
side of the ballroom. When CARLOTTA
has turned her back to her, LUCRETIA
tosses the gifts out of the window.)

LUCRETIA

Whoops.

(CARLOTTA sits on a large chaise lounge,
her fans sitting closely around her.)

PARTY GUEST 2

Carlotta! Do you remember the time
you starred in *Romeo and Juliet*?

CARLOTTA

You know, I had almost completely forgotten all about it!

(She turns to the audience)

Of course I remembered it.

(She turns back to the party.)

You know, Bill himself said that he
wished he could have seen my performance
in his lifetime. It was just brilliant! We had tea together last month,
he's such a delightful gentleman!

PARTY GUEST 3

What was Shakespeare doing all
the way over here, in America?

CARLOTTA

Oh, you know, he's very worldly.

LUCRETIA
(to audience)

Carlotta had never met William Shakespeare.
She was in *Romeo and Juliet* back when
she was in school. She was a tree.

PARTY GUEST 4

Do tell us about the time you
sang at the Queen's Banquet!

PARTY GUEST 1

Oh yes, please do!

CARLOTTA

Surely ya'll don't want to hear me
go on and on about a little bitty
thing like that, now do you?

PICKWICK

Begin with a song! Sing the song
you sang for the queen!

CARLOTTA

Oh, darlins', you wouldn't want
to hear that, would you?

(She is met with cheers and applause. SHE
walks over to the organ and winks at the
ORGANIST, who has clearly been waiting
for this cue. The spotlight shines on
CARLOTTA. She takes a deep breath and pre-
pares to sing. A voice interrupts her.)

CONSTANCE

Happy Death Day, dear Carlotta!

(CONSTANCE stands in the doorway center stage. A flash of lightning is seen and the sound of thunder is heard.)

(BLACKOUT)

(END OF SCENE)

Scene 5

SETTING: The grand ballroom. No one has moved.

AT RISE: CONSTANCE stands in the doorway, and the spotlight has now moved away from CARLOTTA and onto her. The rest of the lighting on stage is dim, and the cast is completely frozen.

CONSTANCE
(to audience)

Another party that I simply wasn't invited to. How dreadful. But, of course, when you all live in the same manor, word spreads quickly. Especially when the word is started by the loudest ghost in the graveyard. So, when sweet little Lucretia dropped a hint about Carlotta's party, I knew I couldn't miss her special day.

(Lights up on the rest of the party scene. The GUESTS are all whispering to each other. CARLOTTA is still frozen in horror.)

CONSTANCE
(to audience)

Oh, you must have heard the rumors by now? Yes, I, Constance Hatchaway, the Merry Murderess, killed not only one, but all

three of my husbands during my lifetime.
Could those horrible accusations be true?

(She laughs.)

Of course they are.

(CONSTANCE looks over to a group
of GUESTS and LUCRETIA, who are
all whispering to each other.)

PARTY GUEST 2

You don't suppose they're actually friends, do you?

LUCRETIA

Carlotta was very selective with her guest
list. Only those invited could attend her
special soiree. Her words, not mine.

PATTY GUEST 3

She actually invited her?

PARTY GUEST 1

I'm not staying much longer if she does.

PARTY GUEST 4

It won't be long until everyone leaves if she's here.

(CONSTANCE laughs again, turning
back to the audience.)

CONSTANCE
(to audience)

It's not that they dislike me. They fear
me. I'm not so sure what they're afraid
of, exactly. It's not like I can kill
any of them. They're already dead.

(CONSTANCE joins the rest of the party, walking straight over to CARLOTTA, who has now pasted her fake smile on her face.)

CARLOTTA

My, my, darlin'! How delightful you came! I was so worried that you wouldn't make it!

CONSTANCE

Well, your invitation was too difficult to pass up. Saying it wouldn't be the same without me. You are too kind!

(They go to give each other a kiss on both cheeks, and whisper to each other, keeping their tones sweet, in case of any eavesdropping.)

CARLOTTA

How dare you show up here, sweet pea.

CONSTANCE

Oh, you really thought I wouldn't? After all the fuss you made, my friend?

CARLOTTA

Who told you about the party, honey?

CONSTANCE

Oh, dear, the manor is not that big. I heard your loud shoes stomping around the ballroom and knew something had to be going on.

(They force a giggle as they turn back to the party.)

CONSTANCE

Now, shouldn't there be dancing?
This is a party, isn't it? Carlotta,
dear, don't tell me you've forgotten how to dance! I know my loving
fiancé will join me for a spin!

(FIANCÉ appears out of the crowd
and stands next to her. The whispers quickly start.)

PARTY GUEST 1

She has a fiancé?!

PARTY GUEST 3

Well, I suppose she can't kill this one.

(CARLOTTA grabs PICKWICK from the crowd.
He is overjoyed at her acknowledge-
ment of him. They stand ready for a
waltz. CARLOTTA glares at CONSTANCE.)

CARLOTTA

Of course, darlin', we were
just waitin' for you!

(The ORGANIST begins to play his
waltz. CARLOTTA pulls PICKWICK
close to her. He is beaming.)

PICKWICK

Carlotta, I've been dreaming of this
all my afterlife. The chance to really
meet you, to dance with you…

(CONSTANCE bumps in to CARLOTTA
as she dances, throwing her off
her step. CONSTANCE laughs.)

PICKWICK

I think we would be quite good
together, you and I. Both of us are
the life of the party after all,
and we have so much in common…

CARLOTTA

Oh, would you stop talking?! I'm
tryin' to listen to her conversation, for goodness' sake!

(CARLOTTA pushes PICKWICK away and grabs
MALE PARTY GUEST and continues dancing.)

CARLOTTA

Thank you for the dance, honey!
So nice of you to save the spot
until my beau could join me!

(PICKWICK falls back, and lands
in LUCRETIA'S arms.)

LUCRETIA

Oh, hello again.

(PICKWICK looks at LUCRETIA, as if
seeing her for the first time.)

PICKWICK

Hello. Lucretia, was it?

LUCRETIA

Yes, that's…

CARLOTTA

LUCRETIA! I NEED TO SEE YOU NOW!

(LUCRETIA tries to ignore her, but
CARLOTTA storms over, pulling the sleeve
of LUCRETIA'S dress. They exit.)

CONSTANCE

Hurry back!

(BLACKOUT)

(END OF SCENE)

Scene 6

SETTING: Outside the ballroom. A long
hallway stretches, with portraits evenly
spaced upon the walls. The portraits seem
to change with every crash of lightning.

AT RISE: CARLOTTA stands, crying hysteri-
cally. LUCRETIA pretends to console her.

CARLOTTA

How could this possibly happen? And to me?
I've certainly done nothin' to deserve such
a mortifyin' experience! I'm a delight!

LUCRETIA

I haven't the faintest idea of how
she could have gotten here. I made
sure to tell everyone not to tell
her, just as you instructed.

CARLOTTA

Then to think, everyone thinks that
I'm the one who invited her! That I'm
friends with that deranged ghoul!

LUCRETIA

I can't imagine…

CARLOTTA

And on my Death Day! It's horri-
fyin'! Oh, I could just die!

LUCRETIA

Well, um, Carlotta, you already have.

CARLOTTA

I can't even wallow in self-
pity in this afterlife!

(CARLOTTA wails in a series of
inaudible sobs. LUCRETIA puts
her arm around CARLOTTA.)

LUCRETIA

There, there. I'm sure once you
explain this horrible tragedy to your
guests, everyone will understand.

(CARLOTTA continues to speak in
sobs. LUCRETIA is patting her
shoulders. She smiles.)

LUCRETIA
(to audience)

Oh, this is just too good.

CARLOTTA

I won't be made a fool! No, that horrible woman will leave at once! And
that'll be the end of it. And you
best ensure that nothin' else goes
wrong at this party, understood?

LUCRETIA

Certainly, Carlotta! I won't let anything else go wrong, I promise
you. I'll fix everything.

CARLOTTA

I deserve the party of the mil-
lennium, not this!

LUCRETIA

Yes, of course you do. Now, deep
breath, and go back in to that party
for all your adoring friends to see!

(CARLOTTA nods, takes a flower
out of LUCRETIA'S hair and puts
it in her own, and exits.)

LUCRETIA
(to audience)

Now, if you were in my shoes, wouldn't
you have done the same? I thought so.

(BLACKOUT)

(END OF SCENE)

Scene 7

SETTING: The ballroom.

AT RISE: CARLOTTA throws the door open.
HARRIET is standing by the piano,
singing to the PARTY GUESTS, who are all
enthralled with her performance. LUCRETIA
follows behind, smiling from ear to ear.

HARRIET
(singing)

"When you hear the knell of a requiem bell, weird glows gleam where spirits dwell. Restless bones etherealize, rise as spooks of every size!"

(CARLOTTA, without hesitation, stands right next to HARRIET, and sings the next line over her.)

CARLOTTA
(singing badly)

"Grim, grinning ghosts come out to socialize!"

(It is now a battle of the divas. The spotlight moves from CARLOTTA to HARRIET as they sing.)

HARRIET
(singing)

"When crypt doors creak and tombstones quake, spooks come out for a swinging wake."

CARLOTTA
(singing badly)

"Happy haunts materialize and begin to vocalize."

BOTH
(singing)

"Grim, grinning ghosts come out to socialize."

(The PARTY GUESTS cheer and applaud as the song comes to an end.)

HARRIET
(to audience)

The applause was all meant for me, of
course. Did you hear Carlotta's voice?
The ghostly cat that lives in the graveyard sounds better than she did, and
I can assure you that a live cat sounds
much better than a dead cat. And to
sing over a world-renowned opera singer.
Well, who does she think she is?

(HARRIET turns back to the PARTY
GUESTS, who are approaching her,
leaving CARLOTTA in the dust.)

CONSTANCE

Dear Harriet! I've never heard such a marvelous rendition of that song. Truly, no
one could possibly sing it better than
you! You simply must sing at our wedding!

(CONSTANCE pulls over FIANCÉ,
who simply nods.)

HARRIET

I'd be honored! Your words are just
too kind. And congratulations to
you both on your engagement!

CONSTANCE

You're the kindest, sweetest ghoul
I've ever met! Thank you.

(CONSTANCE looks over at CARLOTTA,
who is clearly annoyed with all the
praise not directed at her.)

HARRIET

You're so lovely! When's the big day?

CONSTANCE

October 1st, our anniversary!

PARTY GUEST 4

How did you propose?

(Before FIANCÉ can even think about
responding, CONSTANCE is already speak-
ing for him. He looks at the audience,
as if to start his own monologue, but
his speech is quickly interrupted.)

CONSTANCE

He said he simply couldn't live,
for lack of a better word, without
me! Isn't he just the sweetest?

(CONSTANCE shows off her ring, and everyone oohs and awws. CARLOTTA is fuming
with anger, and pushes past her to the
center of the group and smiles.)

CARLOTTA

You know, my dear Wilfred proposed
to me by takin' me on a large river-
boat, rose petals everywhere I looked.
It was divine, he was such a dear.

PARTY GUEST 2

That's nice.

PARTY GUEST 1

Where is Wilfred tonight?

LUCRETIA

Doesn't he spend his days
with his eighth wife?

PARTY GUEST 3
(to another guest)

You wonder why he wouldn't want to
spend it with the great Carlotta?

(Before CARLOTTA can come up with
a clever response, the conversation has already moved on.)

HARRIET

Constance, will it be a big ceremony?

CONSTANCE

It'll be the biggest wedding you've ever
seen! I'm imagining it aboard a large riv-
erboat, rose petals everywhere you look.

PARTY GUEST 1

That sounds like the most roman-
tic thing I've ever heard!

HARRIET

Oh, that's marvelous! I've never
heard of something so lovely!

CARLOTTA

Did ya'll not hear what I just said?

CONSTANCE

Now, now, Carlotta, don't be jealous
just because I've had four wed-
dings and you've only had one!

(Everyone, except CARLOTTA, laughs.
She plasters on a fake smile.)

                    CARLOTTA

        Of course, silly me. Now, let's
        get back to dancin', shall we?

                  PARTY GUEST 3

        Constance, what song will you
          dance to at your wedding?

                    CONSTANCE

      Whatever the Grand Harriet will sing!

                     HARRIET
                  (to audience)

      No one could deny that Constance had
      superb taste in music! Perhaps we had
       misjudged her a bit. I mean, really,
        who could fault her for killing off
       those men? They were men, after all.

         (HARRIET joins the party again.
         CARLOTTA, now clearly pouting,
            pulls CONSTANCE aside.

                    CARLOTTA

        Darlin', I'm sure your weddin'
              will be lovely!

                    CONSTANCE

      Of course it will be. Much better than
     this little excuse for a party, sweetheart.

                    CARLOTTA

      Only in your wildest wishes, suga'.

CONSTANCE

We'll see. But my wedding is more
interesting than your little
party. Isn't that just lovely?

CARLOTTA

I think you're just delusional, sweetie.

(They laugh, noticing a group of
guests who are listening in.)

CONSTANCE

Now, Harriet, would you delight
us all with another song?

HARRIET

But of course! Who would
like to hear another?

(The crowd cheers. In their applause,
CARLOTTA grabs LUCRETIA away from
PICKWICK and pulls her to the side.)

CARLOTTA

I thought you were going to get rid of her!

LUCRETIA

I am! I'm just thinking of the best
way, so it looks like she's leaving
on her own and not forced out.

CARLOTTA
(starting to sob)

I don't care what you do!
Just… Just… do… it…

LUCRETIA
(acting as if the idea just hit her)

I know! I'll go see Madame Leota!
She'll know what to do! Don't you worry,
Carlotta, I'll take care of everything!

(HARRIET begins to sing. CARLOTTA
begins to sob even louder.)

LUCRETIA
(to audience, smiling)

I'll take care of everything.

(BLACKOUT)

(END OF SCENE)

Scene 8

SETTING: Madame Leota's study. It
is very dark, and musical instruments are flying around the room.

AT RISE: MADAME LEOTA sits in
the center of the room, deep in
a trance, her eyes closed.

MADAME LEOTA

Rap on a table, it's time to respond.
Send us a message from somewhere beyond!

(LUCRETIA knocks on the door
and pokes her head in.)

MADAME LEOTA

Enter, young spirit, and say
what you need. But do close the
door, now enter with speed.

(LUCRETIA enters the room, looking at all
the instruments hanging above her head.)

LUCRETIA

Hello, Madame. It's always
a pleasure to see you.

MADAME LEOTA

Dear, sweet, Lucretia, what trouble
you cause. Say what you're here
for, no reason to pause.

LUCRETIA

My plans for Carlotta's party
are going perfectly—

MADAME LEOTA

Through my trance I must speak to all
spirits who dwell, but please answer
the same so I may hear you as well.

LUCRETIA
(to audience)

I love Madame Leota, we all do. She's
the reason we're brought here. Her little
chants call us to the manor. But sometimes
I wish we could have a simple conversation
without all the trouble. And rhyming.

(to Madame Leota)

My plan for the party is working…
so you can see. But I need something bigger…what do I…need?

MADAME LEOTA

A small bit of gossip is not
a strong enough thing, nor one uninvited guest or a diva that sings.

LUCRETIA

Right. That's what… Er, my dear Madame
Leota, you're right, that is true. But
I need a showstopper…something from you?

MADAME LEOTA

I'll send in some mischief, some
ghouls from afar, to add some excitement to make the evening a star.

LUCRETIA

All right, so is that it? Do I go now?
Or do I…slow now? Really, Madame, I'm
running out of rhymes. Times. Limes.

MADAME LEOTA

Hear my instructions, don't leave
in such haste. Just follow my
orders, leave nothing to waste.

LUCRETIA

Oh, so I stay then? Madame, just
tell me what to do. Give me something exciting…something…new?

MADAME LEOTA

In the midst of a fight that you will
lead, a swinging distraction is what
we will need. I'll send in my spirits,
some ghosts that love fun. They'll bring
with them trouble, each and every one.

LUCRETIA

Swinging distraction? I think I can
do that. Thank you, Madame… I'll do it
with…a bat. Not really, I just can't
think of any other rhymes, honestly.

MADAME LEOTA

Now, go, dear Lucretia, and please make
me proud. Make this party a nightmare. Make it big! Make it loud!

(BLACKOUT)

(END OF SCENE)

Scene 9

SETTING:The ballroom.

AT RISE: PICKWICK is sitting atop
the mantle over the fireplace. The
rest of the cast is frozen.

PICKWICK
(to audience)

Let's face it. This party is a complete
disaster. I expected more from the Great
Carlotta, who I had heard so much about.
She promised a great time. And so far,
all I've seen is a party host sobbing
in the corner over every little inconvenience and divas trying to outdo one
another. Perhaps she wasn't the ghoul
I thought she was. And perhaps there
was someone else here this whole time
who had been hidden by her shadow…

(LUCRETIA enters the ballroom.)

LUCRETIA

Pickwick, I need you.

PICKWICK
(to audience)

Well, who can resist when a beautiful ghoul calls you like that?

(LUCRETIA pulls PICKWICK over to her.)

LUCRETIA

What do you say we add a little life to this Death Day?

(They run offstage, whispering as they go. The lights go up on the rest of the scene, showing CARLOTTA still crying in the corner, now with HARRIET comforting her, who is clearly looking for an escape.)

HARRIET

Don't be foolish, Carlotta! This party is wonderful! There's never been such a marvelous 71st Death Day party!

(to audience)

Of course, no one actually celebrates their 71st Death Day.

CARLOTTA

It's just a bona-fide nightmare! It's all that horrible Constance's fault! She's ruined everythin'!

HARRIET

Oh, no, it's not all that bad. She's actually quite lovely.

(This really sets CARLOTTA off. She
storms center, confronting CONSTANCE.
She pulls her stage left, away
from the rest of the party.)

CONSTANCE

Ah, darling! I was wondering when
we would have a dance together!

CARLOTTA

Who told you to be here?! Who was it?

CONSTANCE

You did, my dear! Special invitation came directly from you!

CARLOTTA

I'm not playin' your silly little games
any more. I didn't send you an invitation, so tell me who it was!

(CONSTANCE pulls the invitation
out of a pocket of her dress.)

CONSTANCE

You did.

(CONSTANCE hands CARLOTTA the invitation.
It is signed with her name. CARLOTTA real-
izes that someone did this on purpose.
There is a dead silence in the room.)

CONSTANCE
(to audience)

I truly wish I had just invited myself
to the party and could take all the
credit, really I do. But, when little
Lucretia approached me with her plan

and fake invitation, how could I say no?
Oh, to see the look of pure horror on
Carlotta's face when she opened the invitation, well, that's been worth every
minute of suffering at this awful party.

CARLOTTA

Who sent this to you?!

(LUCRETIA bursts through the door.
She runs straight for CARLOTTA.)

LUCRETIA

Carlotta! I've figured out how
to get rid of Constance!

(She sees CONSTANCE)

Oh. Hello. Um. Oh, this is quite
an awkward situation, isn't it?

CARLOTTA
*(still trying to cover for herself as
she sees her guests approaching)*

Sweet, precious, Lucretia. What could
you possibly be goin' on about now?
Constance is our guest. Why, for Pete's
sake, would we want to get rid of her?

CONSTANCE
(milking it)

I can't believe it! I've never been
so humiliated in my entire life! To
be invited to a party only to be made
a fool and kicked out! How dare you!

(CONSTANCE continues to go on, ad-lib-
bing about how she never expected
this, etc. CARLOTTA talks over her,

explaining that she wants her there.
The GUESTS all begin talking over each
other, taking sides. It is loud, everyone is yelling at everyone. Finally,
one voice is heard over the crowd.)

PICKWICK

Hey! Look up here!

(EVERYONE looks up. PICKWICK is swinging on
a large chandelier over the dance floor.)

CARLOTTA

You get yourself down from there! This
is my moment, not yours! You're ruinin'
this as much as the rest of them!

PICKWICK
(swinging on the chandelier)

Oh, Carlotta. I just wanted to give
you your gift! A REAL PARTY!

(Before CARLOTTA can argue, the
party is flooded with spirits,
filling the ballroom completely.)

CARLOTTA

Who are all these spirits?! Out! Shoo!
All of you! I have a guest list!

(CARLOTTA pulls out the guest list, but
her shrieks are drowned out by the commotion that the spirits are causing. Many
spirits have taken to dancing, hanging on
portraits and bookcases, knocking over
chairs, shooting off firearms. PICKWICK
continues to swing on the chandelier.)

PICKWICK

Look, Carlotta! Your cake is here!

(The CHEF brings the cake over to table. CARLOTTA, who is just hysterical, stands on the chair at the edge of the table to blow out the candles.)

CARLOTTA

If you're at my party, you're at least going to sing to me!

(There is a brief moment of silence, as if they really are going to sing. Instead, everyone laughs and continues what they were doing. CARLOTTA sighs and tries to blow out her candles. They light again. She tries a second time. They light themselves again. This happens one more time.)

CARLOTTA

I can't even blow out my candles! Why does everythin' always have to happen to me!?

LUCRETIA

You're just lucky that way, I suppose!

(BLACKOUT)

(END OF SCENE)

Scene 10

SETTING: The ballroom. Everything is now a mess, with food all over the tables, decorations torn off the walls, and furniture turned over. Most of the guests have left.

AT RISE: CARLOTTA sits at her chair at the edge of the table, pouting. Her candles

on the cake are still lit. LUCRETIA and
PICKWICK are sitting downstage left,
whispering to each other and smiling.
CONSTANCE walks over to CARLOTTA.

CONSTANCE

You must admit, it was quite a party.

CARLOTTA

A bunch of hitchhikin' hooligans
think they can come in to my party
and take over. They didn't even wish
me a happy Death Day, you know.

CONSTANCE

Carlotta, dear, no one but you celebrates their 71st Death Day. It's
about time someone told you that.

CARLOTTA

Oh, do I really need an excuse to
gather friends together to celebrate my life? I should think not!

CONSTANCE

Well, next time, consider actually
inviting the one person that stayed to
help you clean up the party, maybe?

(CARLOTTA stops to think. She doesn't
want to admit it, but she knows she's
right. She uncrosses her arms.)

CARLOTTA

You're right. For my 72nd Death
Day celebration, all 999 Happy
Haunts get the invitation.

CONSTANCE

And, of course, we'll pretend that
I still wasn't invited, and no one will
ever know about this conversation.

CARLOTTA

Absolutely not! We'll still bicker
with each other as we always have.
However, if I'm not invited to your
weddin', I'll just be arrivin' anyway.

CONSTANCE

I wouldn't have it any other way.

(They laugh.)

CARLOTTA

Now, skedaddle, before anyone sees
us actually gettin' along.

(They both smile at each other, and
CONSTANCE exits the stage. PICKWICK and
LUCRETIA stand, and exit behind her,
hand in hand. CARLOTTA is left alone
on the stage. She looks around, smiles,
and finally, blows out her candles.)

(BLACKOUT)

(END OF SCENE)

Scene 11

SETTING: Madame Leota's study.
The instruments have now vanished, leaving her alone.

AT RISE: MADAME LEOTA sits center,
a spotlight shining on her.

MADAME LEOTA
(to audience)

Throughout the years, no one could agree, on what happened that night, on what they did see. Each ghost and ghoul claims a different end, on who walked away foe and who walked away friend.

The party is over, our story is told. A tale for mortals to enjoy, both the young and the old. And while mischief and mayhem are what we do best, we leave it to you, yes, here is the rest. Our story doesn't end here inside our little dome. It continues with you, as a ghost will follow you home!

(BLACKOUT)

(END OF ACT)

Mine for the Taking

a Frontierland short story by Patrick Kling

Deep over yonder in the far reaches of the frontier, gold was bein' struck all across the West. The so called "gold rush" brought thugs, cut-throats, deadbeats, tricksters, low-lifes, rough riders, and a few good pioneers out to the untamed West. Overnight, one of these folks might strike it rich in Middle of Nowhere, U.S.A. Once gold was struck in an area, prospectors, miners, and whiners would pour into the land faster than a base burner flowin' into a bender. They'd dig into the rocks, the mountains, the hills, and the caves.

Things didn't often go to plan in these mines. Rustic trains, dangerous explosives, and calamitous caverns made every day a thrill for workers, prospectors, and the families of these folks. The results led to transient "get-rich-quick" types, grazin' over the land with no respect to inhabitants, both indigenous dwellers and local wildlife. A common story.

However, our tale is not so common. It took took place in the humble boomtown of Tumbleweed. Decades prior, the town had sprung up around the Big Thunder Mining Company, owned by the infamous Barnabas T. Bullion. Like most boom towns, it had seen better days. When the mine was first commissioned in the early 1850s, there was plenty of gold. It was a happenin' place for those fixin' to make a quick buck and have a good time while doin' it.

Out of all those who fled to this area, the most ruthless by a long shot was Barnabas T. Bullion. You'll see what I mean a bit later. His family got the rights to the lands once a bit of sparkle was found by a travelin' pioneer headin' west to Frisco. That pioneer tried to stake his claim, but the government intervened and granted those land rights to the Barnabas family. That humble pioneer was never to be heard from again.

He may have gotten the last laugh, though, as once minin' started, unexpected things happened. The local indigenous Indians warned Barnabas that Thunder Mountain was protected by their ancestors, and not to be excavated or bothered with in any way. Naturally, the all-knowin' Yankees *knew* better, or so they thought.

It started off simple. A few minor tremors here and there, dynamite that wouldn't explode, and shovels and pickaxes that would fall apart after first use. Negligible, really, an annoyance to the bottom line, until the incident happened.

The ground shook in the first shaft, causin' a cave-in at the entrance. Just a handful of miners were in the pocket at the time. Those outside tunneled into the pocket to save their trapped fellows within mere minutes, but they had vanished without a trace. No equipment, no bodies, no evidence of anythin' ever bein' in that shaft. Barnabas did everythin' he could to cover up the story. He bribed all those who had tunneled to save their trapped brethren. Nevertheless, rumors began to swirl, and it spooked the crew.

Those who were skeptical and loyal to Barnabas were thrust into the havoc of the Big Thunder Mine. Flash floods, earthquakes, tumblin' rocks, and even runaway ghost trains met them, all at the hands of those legendary Indian spirits. Barnabas had lost his handle on it, and word spread throughout the Wild West that Big Thunder Mine was haunted and dangerous. The turnover rate was fierce. All this havoc caused the mine to be a bungled boondoggle.

That brings us to the day this tale truly begins. Over 30 years had passed, and Barnabas still wouldn't let go. He had seemingly unlimited resources from his family, but his most allegiant team was stretched thin. He was fixin' to find a solution once and for all, and called a meetin' of his directors with the intention of squashin' any worries. This company was going to keep runnin' until there was nothin' left of the mountain to dig! Twelve of them had assembled in the boardroom of the minin' office, along with Barnabas' trusty number two, Austin Arlurton.

"Thank you for coming today on such short notice," Austin said. The directors kept chattin' amongst themselves.

"Excuse me, order, order." he said. The fellers kept talkin'.

The door slammed open, with Barnabas stompin' in, takin' his spot at the head of the table. Everyone leapt to their feet and stood at attention. He gave them a nod, givin' permission for them to sit down.

"Many of you may have heard, discussed, desired, or even *demanded* that it is time to for us to pack up this mining operation," Barnabas bellowed. "If any of you believe it is time to shut down, please raise your hand."

Weatherby Johnson rose his hand. "Sir, we're overworked, we ain't findin' any gold, and the crew is too spooked to be productive."

"Weatherby, you've been by my side for nearly 30 years, right at the beginning," Barnabas softly responded. Weatherby nodded.

"I have always trusted your judgment and your advice. We've spent countless nights over the years keeping this company alive. Go ahead and stand up and to the front and tell us more."

Weatherby stayed seated.

"Go ahead, come on up and tell us what you propose. We need solutions here. Many lives depend on it."

Relieved, Weatherby obliged and walked toward the front of the room. Barnabas reached his hand out for a hand shake. As they clenched hands for the shake, Barnabas grabbed Weatherby's shoulder and threw him out the window. He plummeted, screamin' the entire way. If you ask me, it was his sleep deprivation that had led him to be so foolish to aim to please ol' man Bullion.

"Is there anybody else? Anybody here that thinks it's time to close up?" Barnabas asked.

The room was completely silent. You could've heard a pin drop all the way over at the Gold Dust Saloon.

"Very good. Now, I need you all to get back to that dang mine and get more gold from your teams!"

His directors ran out of the room. Barnabas and Austin marched to Barnabas' corner office in a fiery flurry. Austin slammed the door behind them.

"Who do these *yokels* think they are? Questioning you like that? We could have them tarred and feathered by dawn with your approval, sir."

"Austin," Barnabas said softly, "they're right."

"No! We can still get at least another twenty-five tons of gold out of this mine."

Austin had dedicated nearly twenty years of his life to Barnabas. He had worked his way up through the ranks as an explosives expert, then to a driveman, on to an equipment handler and then a crew lead. Barnabas began groomin' him once he heard rumors of the ruthless manager who put the company's needs ahead of its workers' well being. That was just how Barnabas liked it. However, Austin was now focused on his next steps. He dreamed of runnin' his own operation one day, maybe even Big Thunder Mine itself.

Barnabas stood silently for a moment. Austin was clearly anxious to know what would happen next. "It's time to implement plan '92," Barnabas triumphantly proclaimed.

"What's tha—" Austin began.

"Let me finish, you twit. Number '92' has been my backup plan since the beginning. We need to prospect Chick-A-Pin Hill. Once we figure out what's inside of the mountain, we'll mine it for *everything* its got."

"Chick-A-Pin Hill? We can hardly get miners down in *these* corridors, and you want to mine Chick-A-Pin Hill?! That hill has rushing waters flowing through it, along with *dangerous* animals. You're daft!"

"I'm daft, alright, daft like a fox," Barnabas replied with a grin. "We need to assemble a team, and we need the best prospector in the West."

Austin looked confused for a moment, then frowned. "No, sir! I am far more qualified to lead this prospecting mission than Ginny."

"You're right, Austin. You are actually *overqualified* to lead this mission. This mine needs you. You are an important member of this team."

Barnabas was lyin', of course. He'd recently grown weary over how ambitious his number two had been. Many leaders would groom someone and be happy for their success. Barnabas didn't see it that way. He wanted Austin to work tirelessly forever for him. Any type of dissension or free thinkin' could lead to disaster. He wasn't exactly sure who'd rustled his directors' feathers up recently. Could it have been Austin himself? Barnabas always stayed one step ahead.

"Ginny should be passing through town for the summer festival. Go find her and get her to sign up for this expedition. Can you handle that, Austin?"

"Of course. I'll get a team together, and we'll rope Ginny into this."

Ginny Bigbsy was one of the most illustrious prospectors in the West, though I reckon the term "prospector" doesn't do her justice. She was tough, rough, and smart, and could sell dirt to a miner. She roamed the West seekin' to help those in need, defeat those creatin' havoc, and to aid her fellow pioneers. Adventure, and more importantly trouble, had a way of findin' her wherever she roamed.

She was travelin' with her trusty horse, Sugarbits. She had gotten an early start, and was already in the heart of town by high noon, her favorite time of day. A few townspeople cheered as she moseyed her way toward the Gold Dust Saloon to meet her brother Boone for lunch.

Boone's story was an interestin' one. He had joined the Big Thunder Mining Company about a decade prior. He was one part engineer, one part tinkerer, one part coward. You heard me right, the apples fell quite far apart between him and his slick, big sis Ginny. Despite his cowardice, he worked hard to keep the crews safe by inventin' all sorts of fancy equipment. The latest fan belts, or canary cages that would work above ground, or longer, safer fuses. If he could dream it up in his silly brain, he could do it. He was in a perpetual pickle, though. Boone would constantly reinvest all his money into further inventions that would only benefit Barnabas T. Bullion himself. It goes without sayin' that Barnabas took advantage of this, and he'd make Boone pay for all of his materials while he reaped all the benefits. He'd charge him for dynamite, bricks, sticks, pencils, and even dirt. Boone was in a revolvin' debt with Barnabas and had no way out. Now that yer acquainted with Boone, let's get back to the meat of our story.

Ginny burst through the swingin' door to the saloon, and her arrival was rejoiced by all the patrons.

"Ginny!" they all shouted.

Ginny smiled with a keen nod and stomped over to *her* table, center stage. There was excitement in the air, as news was spreadin' throughout town that she was back. They brought over her usual, a shot of whiskey. It was all on the house. She always insisted on paying, but her money seemed to be good nowhere, nohow.

Shortly after her grand arrival, Boone clumsily knocked open the swingin' doors of the saloon. They knocked him in the rear as they swung shut behind him. He was holdin' some new doohickey in his hands. He stumbled through the room, knockin' into patrons and fumblin' into chairs. He and Ginny gave each other a big ol' hug.

"Boone, how the heck are ya?"

They took their seats at the table.

"Listen, Ginny, I have some news. Ol' man Barnabas is gonna try and rope you into some crazy ill-gotten plan to raid Chick-A-Pin Hill. You better say no. The legends...the legends of that mountain are...."

"Chick-A-Pin Hill, eh?" she coyly responded. "Sounds like adventure to me."

"No, no, no. You shouldn't work for that ol' kook. Once you work for him, he'll rope you into all sorts of trouble, and you'll owe him for the rest of yer life."

"I can take care of Barnabas. I am fixin' to get you out of this Thunder Mountain nightmare. You should be tinkerin' elsewhere, makin' it big at the Expos in Chicagi'. And of course, helpin' yer younger sister with fandangled doodads, to help her on her adventures." There was a plan brewin' in her melon.

"Well, I'd love nothin' more but—" Boone began.

"Boone, it's time you stick up for yerself . We're gonna get through this together. You'll be with me every step of the way."

"Ol' man Barnabas ain't gonna let us work together."

"Leave that to me," she said with a smile.

The gizmo Boone was holdin' shook violently.

"Now what in tarnation is that doodad in your hand?"

"It's my latest and greatest invention yet! It's able to alert miners when there's an earthquake nearby," he replied as confident as he could muster.

And by gum, he was right! Not a moment went by before Betsy Dalourie came scamperin' up to Ginny's table. Betsy was the nightly headliner. She was a diamond in the rough, and tough as the ol' West. She had a smile that would crack a hole in gold itself. Ginny and her had a fondness for one another. (Now it wouldn't be prudent for me to dive further into those details. I am sure you understand.)

"Betsy!" Ginny said with the biggest smile she had donned in a long while. She gave her a big hug and lifted her off her heels. The moment was short-lived.

"News is spreadin' throughout town that Barnabas is fixin' to proposition you on a horrid mission. Promise me you won't go. I would be a mess without you."

"Now, Betsy, I will always be there for you, don't you worry. No need to get your knickers in a bunch, I promise."

"Well, then, I am comin' with ya! I could be of assistance," Betsy stated with charmin' confidence.

"I work alone. I can't get anybody else roped in on this."

"You were gonna drag *me* into this, Ginny," Boone whispered.

"Thanks for the reminder, Boone. I had almost forgotten." She turned and said to Betsy, "This could be far too dangerous, trust me on this one."

She was interrupted by Austin sneakin' up behind her.

"Ginny, is that you? It has been far too long. Mind if I take a seat?"

"Why, yes, as a matter of fact I do. And how dare you not address Betsy and Boone here."

"Afternoon, ma'am. Boone, howdy," Austin stated with as much pride as he could muster. "I'm here to talk to you about a proposition. It's top secret, though, so we need to discuss it in private."

"I'm listenin'." Ginny had no intention of wheelin' and dealin' with Austin. She wanted to talk straight with Barnabas.

"You're here to proposition her to lead an expedition to Chick-A-Pin Hill, and she's got better things to do than somethin' like this!" Betsy said.

"Is this true, Ginny? You're not interested?" Austin asked. "Well, I completely understand. I am sure we'll find someone more capable of handlin' this situation."

She merely shrugged as he headed toward the door. It was a rather pitiful demonstration. There was a bit of a scuffle heard outside the bar, a loud shout followed by a splash in the nearby horse trough.

The scuffle concluded with Barnabas slammin' his way through the door, marchin' to Ginny's table. Austin was dryin' off nearby. That horse spit smell can be difficult to wash out.

"Ginny! What a great surprise to have your great presence in our humble town," he stated.

"Howdy, Mr. Bullion."

"Oh no, no, you must call me Barnabas! Please, may I take a seat?"

"Of course, Barnabas."

Barnabas snapped his fingers and the bartender appeared with two glasses and a bottle of whiskey.

"I always like a shot before talking business," he stated.

He filled up both glasses and took two shots with a chuckle. Ginny, without missin' a beat, guzzled her drink and grabbed the whisky bottle and gave it a swig. She slammed it on the table. Barnabas filled up her glass, and she took another shot.

"Ginny, you're the long-lost daughter I never had." He was impressed, and I reckon you are, too. "I am going to get straight to the point, I know Austin had a chat with you, but failed to get the details right."

"I know what you want. The question is, what's in it for me?" Ginny replied. She was always in charge.

"A straight shooter, I love it! What'll it be?"

"Well, let's see. First things first, if I do this for you, I want you to forgive all loans my brother owes you and your company."

"Well, I can't do that.... He owes far too much for a silly mission like this! We can get another to lead this mission. Is there anything else I can offer you?"

Ginny poured herself another shot of whisky, drank it, and slammed the glass to the floor.

"Thanks for the drinks," she said, colder than than a desert winter's night, as she trotted toward the door.

Not to be outmatched, Barnabas took out his six-shooter and fired a round upwards to the ceilin'. The entire bar fell silent, as Ginny, unfazed, continued to walk toward the swingin' saloon doors.

"Dagnabit, Ginny, *fine*," Barnabas said, "his debt will be forgiven."

Ginny paused in her tracks, the entire bar still silent.

"That's a good start," she said coyly. She spun around and casually walked back to the table.

"That's all I can do," Barnabas stated firmly.

"I told you it was just a start, and I meant it. "You don't think *Austin* could actually handle this for you. He couldn't find sarsaparilla at a soda fountain, let alone save your ill-gotten mine."

Barnabas was frustrated but powerless. He wasn't used to bein' told no. He hadn't gotten this far in life without controllin' his temper a bit.

"Let's hear your terms," he reluctantly whispered.

"I need a crew. A couple of henchman and my brother Boone."

"Fine."

"And one more thing. If I do this mission, and I don't find anythin', I need your word that you'll look into contingency plans to shut down this horrid Thunder Mountain Mine once and for all," she stated, a half bluff.

"You're out of your mind! I ain't letting some benevolent hick tell me how to run my company—" he fiercely stated.

"I'm not done. The plan must ensure all townspeople are given the chance to make a better life wherever you wander to next," Ginny said. She sure was pushin' for a lot.

"Absolutely not!" Barnabas screamed so loud it would have woken up a deaf man.

He grabbed the bottle of whisky and threw it to the ground.

Of course, without skippin' a beat, Ginny took out her trusty flask, took a shot of whisky, and made her way toward the door with Betsy and Boone followin' closely behind.

Barnabas was silent. Patrons of that fine establishment started to whisper. Had this ol' baron met his match?

"I want to go with you two,"Betsy pleaded once they got outside.

"You heard Barnabas. Looks like the deal is off," Ginny said with a grin.

"I wasn't born yesterday, Ginny, I know you got this covered."

"It's no negotiation. It's not the right mission. I will get you along for anotha' one, I promise. Not this time," she firmly said.

Ginny and Boone hopped on their horses and rode straight to Boone's home. It was a fantastic sight to see, a humble barn of sorts jam-packed with all sorts of doodads and gizmos linin' the place from floor to ceilin'. It would've make you question your own smarts, I reckon. He had a contraption that would boil an egg, a doohickey that would detect gold in the strangest of places, and lots of other devices, too.

Boone slowly walked into his workshop and stared at a set of fancy equations on the blackboard. He paused for a moment, then grabbed a piece of chalk and crossed things off quicker than a six-shooter at a duck hunt.

"It's wrong! It's all wrong! This contraption is completely worthless," Boone said. He was talkin' 'bout his tremor invention. He threw it on a stack of his other failed inventions. However, his philosophy was a prudent one. Every failure was a lesson leadin' him to a success. Bright words from a bright man.

Ginny sat on a stool near his workbench. She enjoyed takin' it all in. You see, while his primary focus was on minin', he'd moonlight developin' all sorts of contraptions for Ginny to use on her adventures. Boone ruffled through a stack of papers, just before he wrestled with a devilish doodad never before seen by the sane. It had three dials on it, was made of copper, and had a long rope danglin' to the floor.

"This is my latest and greatest! Here, take it!" he exclaimed.

She grabbed the doohickey by what appeared to be a handle. She carelessly twisted a knob launchin' a hook mere inches away from poor Boone's head. The hook was attached to a rope, that was attached to the gizmo.

"I call it 'Boone's Rope Hook,'" he stated proudly.

"That has to be the dumbest name for somethin' I'd ever heard," she said with a teasing grin. Boone ignored her.

"You see, you aim with the handle, point the hook upward. If a miner gets trapped in a mine shaft, they can use this to get out! It can lift even the fattest pigs of the bunch!"

"Very impressive; you better bring this for our expedition to Chick-A-Pin Hill. You never know what type of holes we may end up in."

"But I thought we weren't goi...."

Just at that very moment, an alarm bell went off. A scream was heard, pleadin' for dear life itself.

"Help! Cut me down this instant!"

Ginny gave Boone a nod. They'd better investigate. She was on high alert. Sure, she was a hero. But there are always villainous types out there tryin' to take her down.

"It's comin' from the north field," Boone said. He got out a handy pair of fancy binoculars, peeked through the window, and began to chuckle once he saw what was caught up in his trap.

"Take a look," he said with a grin.

She was relaxed, seein' his expression. "Well, well, we've got a live one, I reckon," she stated with the snark bit of humor she was known and loved for.

Boone covered up a few of his gizmos and plans with a tarp and followed Ginny out to the north field. There was the captive, screamin' and flailin' in the wind, caught in a net upside down.

"Help me! Let me down!" he said as he squirmed. It was a sight to see, it really was.

"Now, Austin, you know trespassin' is a crime in these here parts," Ginny said with a forced stern face. Yup, it was that feller Austin.

"This type of trap should be illegal! I could have been killed!"

Ginny gave Boone a nod, then took out a knife and cut him down. He hit the floor with a thud. He brushed the dirt and leaves from his hair. He looked like a pig in a sty.

"So, it looks like Barnabas agrees to my terms, I reckon?" Ginny stated with her humble Western charm.

"Yes," Austin said with a whisper as he regained his composure.

"Even the contingency plan? Everyone would get relocated?"
"Yes!"

"And my crew? Where's my crew?"

"Well, Ginny, your'e looking at it."

"Yer kiddin'! I don't have time to mess around with the likes of you. Now seriously, where is my crew?"

"Barnabas needs someone out there that he can trust, and frankly, he can't trust you. I don't trust you," Austin stated as he moved closer. Ginny gave him a look that could melt the sun. He halted in his tracks like a railroad out of steam.

"Welp, a deal's a deal. I failed to specify who would come on this expedition, therefore I will take anyone, even you," she stated softly as she moved closer to Austin.

She slyly grabbed his collar and fixed it straight. He signed in relief. He was nervous. She got even closer.

"Austin, I don't trust you, but what I do need you to know is that I have everyone's back. If you are on my crew, I have your back. Can you give me your word you have mine?"

"Absolutely. This is strictly business."

"Alright. This pathetic peace party is over, time to get a move on," she said.

"Are you crazy? It's almost sundown, no reason to leave now."

"I agree, Ginny, this doesn't seem like a good idea, goin' out and wanderin' in the middle of the night, across the plains," Boone said, addin' to the confusion.

"We've been dilly-dadlin' all day! You fellas act like you've never been on an adventure before. Now, let's roll. *Now!*" She whistled for Sugarbits. "Meet me at the Butterfly Stage Line in twain," she screamed as she rode off over yonder. (Oh, you'll have to excuse me, "twain" is our simple word for "two.")

Boone and Austin frantically raced to their respective homes. Boone packed up a few gadgets and a day pack, while Austin made for Big Thunder Mining Co. to give Barnabas the news and pack up a pack.

Ginny trotted along to meet Colonel T.B. Clydesdale himself, who'd prepared their late evenin' carriage. Sugarbits warmed up to the horses quickly and shared some horse feed and water. Colonel T.B. and Ginny were long-time friends. He'd actually found Sugarbits for her, and she had rescued him time and time again from crooks and thieves out on the prairie.

"Now, I know what yer up to out there, Ginny. And I'm worried about ya. I've heard stories about that Chick-A-Pin

Hill. About country critters up in there, pioneers gettin' eaten, or worse, goin' mad," Colonel T.B. said in warning. Ginny wasn't too worried about all that, though.

"You don't *really* believe in all that superstition, do you?"

"Ginny, you've seen loonier stuff over the West more so than I. I reckon ya best keep yer wits about ya," Colonel T.B. proclaimed. He wasn't all caught up in the glory of Ginny.

"Yer right, I'll keep my...." Ginny began.

"And I don't trust that goofy Austin neither. Ya better keep him on a tight leash. He'd double-cross ya faster than ol' Betsy's legs durin' her can-can routine."

"Why you bringin' Betsy into this, T.B.?" she said as she gave him a playful poke to the ribs.

They shared a good laugh. She threw her pack onto the stage coach and greeted Boone as he approached the carriage. Sugarbits was tied up to lead the pack, and T.B. was mannin' the reigns.

"That's been twain, let's go!" Ginny shouted. Boone hurried into the carriage while Ginny hopped up with the colonel.

"Yeehaw!" she screamed as the horses neighed and trotted toward the evenin' stars. In the distance, Austin could be heard screamin'.

"Wait! Wait, you daft ol' fools!"

They slowed down the horse just enough so he could catch up.

"I said *twain*, Austin. Yer not off to a good start. Now get on or get off!" Ginny said with as much rustic charm as you could pack in a valley.

He hobbled his way into the carriage, throwin' his bag clumsily on the roof. Boone gave him a rightful chuckle and a light dustin'.

"It's better to listen to her than get on her bad side," Boone warned.

"I thought I was *already* on her bad side."

"No, yer not. You're more in the middle."

Austin shrugged it off and stared out the window. Ginny and T.B. spent a spell catchin' up on all her adventures throughout the frontier. Yup, it was a great, big, beautiful land of the frontier.

It was gettin' a bit late. They had made it quite a few miles down the rustic path, and were now travelin' through a bit of a forest. Chick-A-Pin Hill could be seen in the distance. Ginny was now ridin' in the coach with the fellers, restin' up and catchin' a wink.

Austin peered at the moonlight lightin' up the peak of that hill like it was the spotlight of the midnight revue at the ol' Gold Dust Saloon. He gave a menacin' grin. Boone took notice.

"What are you so grinful about over there?"

"I've been wanting to conquer that Chick-A-Pin Hill for decades. I've been bidin' my time to run my own mining operation."

Ginny opened an eye. "You mean, runnin' it for ol' man Bullion, right, Austin?"

"Of course, of course, for Barnabas," he said, fumbling for his composure.

"Don't get all excited about *conquerin'* anything. If yer gonna be one with the land, you must be at peace with it. The land isn't to be conquered. It's to be preserved, shared, and yes, if ya need resources you may take what ya need. Those superstitions out there are more than superstitions. It's energy."

"Ah, phooey, Ginny, you don't believe all that nonsense. I know yer reputation."

"Easy now, fellers, stay focused," Boone whispered.

There was a bit of slowin' down of the carriage. It was half past midnight. Boone shifted slightly, while Austin lit up a smoke. The wind started to howl and a fierce breeze blew out Austin's cigarette. The sounds of whispers could be heard shufflin' amongst the trees.

Somethin' wasn't right, voices could be heard in unison: *Stay away....*

The horses neighed and halted, causin' the carriage to bump. Austin's eye lit up. He reached for his pistol.

The horses were spooked and with that halt, a trunk fell to the ground.

"*OW!*" someone screamed from within.

Ginny hopped down to the ground grabbin' her six-shooter, ready for action. T.B. hopped down, too.

"Wait, wait!" he pleaded.

Ginny shot off the trunk's hinges which had been damaged in the crash, and sure enough Betsy Dalourie herself rolled out, gaspin' for a bit of fresh air.

Ginny turned to T.B., lookin' for answers.

"She really wanted to come," he stated with a bit of sorrow. Ginny shook her head and went to Betsy's aid.

"I'm fine, just a bit out of breath." She was proud, aimin' to prove herself to be a trusty side-splitin' sidekick.

"Yer not fine, you look like yer dressed for the midnight revue! I explicitly told you not to come! I can't be babysittin' *one* of you folks, let alone three!" She was brutal but had a point.

'Well, I'm stickin' with you and that's that."

"That's that, huh?"

T.B. said, "I can't take you any farther. You're not too far away from the base of the mountain. I'll let you off here, y'all should camp out where its a bit safer, but I gotta get my horses away before it too late."

"Don't be a fool, you ol' kook," Austin said. He headed straight to the horses to attempt to rein them in.

"I wouldn't do that if I were you," Ginny said.

Austin never paid no mind, and charged up behind the horse. He grabbed one of the reins and was promptly met with a kick from Sugarbits' hind leg launchin' him several feet into the air. He was knocked out cold.

"Thanks, T.B., for the ride. We'll take it from here," Ginny said.

They unloaded the carriage full of provisions and supplies, and started a fire to keep warm.

"Be safe, and 'member what I told ya," T.B. bellowed as he made his way back through the trees.

"What did he tell you?" Betsy muttered.

"No matter now."

Betsy and Ginny stayed close to one another, while Boone set up a few handy traps and alarms to ensure they could rest easy, at least for the night.

It was mornin' now, with Austin still knocked out. They packed up their supplies and loaded them neat and tight on Sugarbits' saddle. But, it was time to wake up Austin. With the ol' heave ho, they lifted him up and threw him in a nearby stream. That did the trick. He screamed, gaspin' for air.

"*I can't swim!* I'm drowning!" He flailed his arms wildly in the mornin' sun.

"Austin, sta...." Ginny began.

"You'll pay for this! Help me!"

"Austin, all you need to do is sta...." Betsy said, gettin' in on it, too. They couldn't believe it, a man thinkin' he was drownin' in a no more than a few inches of water.

"We don't have time for this," Ginny said as she grabbed him by the collar.

"Just. Stand," she said.

Boone and Betsy had a good laugh as Austin made his way to his feet. Curiously, even a little rabbit, along with a bear and a fox, seemed to chuckle along with 'em.

"Nap time is over, time to head out!" Ginny commanded as she saddled up onto Sugarbits.

"I'm far too rattled from that devilish horse of yers kickin' me. I can't walk," Austin whined.

"Better get crawlin,' then," Ginny blurted without skippin' a beat.

She gave Betsy a hand and pulled her up onto the horse with her. They rode off with Boone and Austin followin' behind.

It was only a half day's journey, but somethin' strange happened. The closer they got, the more clouds seemed to form around that mountain. They were quick to take notice.

"Must be decades since anybody came to Chick-A-Pin Hill," Betsy said.

"I heard a brute once came here, and he was never heard from again. His name was Slicky Willy. Well, I guess it was," Boone said drearily.

"Okay, Boone, that's enough. Stay close, we are almost to the base. I can see it just up ahead," Ginny said.

With the clouds formin', it got darker and darker. Too dark to even see what was mere steps in front of 'em. The travelers grew weary. You'd be too, I reckon.

"Ginny, we better set up camp for the night," Austin said, musterin' up a bit of confidence through his dread.

"This'll work. We have a stream right over there that will

supply us with fresh water. However, need I remind you that it is barely past noon."

"R-r-right," he replied.

Just then, some hissin' was heard from behind the brush, and ol' Austin jumped out of his boots! He grabbed his hat that had fallen and grabbed a stick. He banged against the rocks to scare whatever *it* was away. Ginny gave Boone a nod and he unbuckled his satchel and unloaded one of his contraptions. It was an alarm of sorts. He placed a series of string across the perimeter of their camp. Any intruders would trigger it, alertin' them with a loud bell. It made them feel a bit safer as the animal sounds grew just a bit louder.

"There sure are a lot of animals in these here parts," Betsy whispered.

They set up a fire for a bit of a light and were gathered around.

"That's what happens when pioneers haven't had a chance to scare em or kill 'em all. It's a beautiful thing, really. The way we can live with the animals if we weren't foolish with our resources," Ginny said with a bit of passion. Sugarbits gave off a knowin' neigh. They had a connection, they sure did.

Ginny commanded, "Don't get too comfortable, it's time we get on with the mission at hand. Betsy, you stay here with Austin and watch the camp. We'll need you to keep an eye out for anythin' out of the ordinary. I may be suspicious of those tall tales, but there ain't no reason we should let our guard down.

"But I wanna go with ya!"

"You're needed here. The first lesson of bein' an adventurer is understandin' that everyone has a role and every role is important."

"I'll keep you nice and warm, Betsy," Austin stated, creepier than the town drunk at the midnight revue.

Ginny jumped into action and threw her handy knife straight at Austin's body. It sliced his pantaloons and pinned him to the log his was sittin' on.

"You could've killed me!"

Ginny approached Austin to retrieve her knife.

"Say somethin' like that again, and I will," she whispered in his ear.

Things were gettin' fierce. They had a bit of history, and it showed. Boone was stopped in his tracks. He wasn't used to all this frontier violence. They departed camp and headed for the summit.

"You know, I could've killed him if I wanted," Ginny said, feelin' the need to explain.

"And what that have proved? You would have been arrested for murder. You can't kill a man based on his words!"

"It's a good thing he didn't move, then," Ginny chuckled. She could find the humor in the most extreme circumstances.

They hiked and hiked up toward the top of that mountain. It felt endless to them, even though they used a few of Boone's inventions to help them climb. It was not a hospitable climb, not one bit. Jagged rocks, steep drop offs, and rushin' water all over the place. It's any wonder they hadn't slipped and fell down the river.

"I think we are just far enough to talk business. You see how treacherous this here mountain is, water splashin' everywhere. There's a spring up at the top. If they mine this mountain, it's gonna damage the animal life for hundreds of miles," Ginny said as a plan was bein' cooked up in her melon.

"B-b-but...." Boone muttered.

"Leave that to me. We need to make it look like we've tried to find soil. We "grab" a few samples around the mountain and then we take it back to ol' man Barnabas and tell 'em there ain't nothin' to mine."

"It could work...." Boone agreed.

Ginny heard a scream echoin' across the mountain.

"It's Betsy! We gotta get down the mountain!" she shouted at Boone. She rummaged to collect her gear and grabbed the Boone Rope Hook.

She shot it toward the lower rocks and swung down.

"Wait!" Boone pleaded.

She was already gone, nothin' but dust by that point. She swung down and around faster than you could ever imagine. Over those jagged rocks, those spikes, those gaps. She navigated them all with pure precision. She heard the scream again, as animals could be heard rummagin' in the nearby trees.

"I'm comin', Betsy!"

She jumped over streams, ponds, and waterfalls. Gettin' closer, she sprinted through the forest at the base of the mountain. The fire was out, but she could see the smolderin' above the trees.

Gettin' closer, she came upon Betsy, in hysterics.

"They took him, I-I-I...." Betsy began.

"Who took him?"

"Th-the animals," she said, exasperated more than you know.

"How could they take him? Did they kill him?"

"No, no, much worse!"

"Worse?!"

"He went daft! I went to explore the river a bit with Sugarbits and when we came back he had hundreds of critters all around him! He was *enchanted* by them. I stayed out of the limelight, and saw him in some kind of a trance walk out straight into the forest. It was the strangest thing...." She was scared.

"That don't make no sense, Betsy, yer pullin' my lariat." She'd seen all sorts of things out there in the West, but a bunch of animals enchantin' a man is somethin' she'd never heard of. "Okay, Betsy, lets get you a drink of water. I'm sure he'll come back."

"We have to go find him. I don't want him to die, not like that."

"Alright, alright, Betsy, I agree. Let's take a minute to get our wits about us. Boone should be comin' any minute now." Ginny had a heart. She really did intend to save ol' Austin.

All the animal noises they'd been hearin' were long gone. Now, an hour had gone by and there was no sign of Boone. Ol' Ginny was a bit worried by now, but naturally had a plan.

"Betsy, yer comin' now, if I know anythin' about my brother, I am sure he's caught up in whatever mess Austin's in."

"Oh no, Ginny, you don't think they got Boone, too, do you?" Betsy said with compassion.

"Betsy, the second rule to bein' a frontier adventurer is ya can't get distracted. I've been in peril countless times, and you have to use your compassion to stay focused." Ginny was always lookin' for a lesson. "Let's get on, we'll trace the tracks through the forest."

They gathered a few provisions and hopped onto Sugarbits. Ginny gave her a nice rub on the neck and pointed her onwards to track the scent. She made haste through the forest, trottin' right through all obstacles in the way. As they approached a thick brush, animals began squeakin', squawkin', and chirpin'. There had to be animals nearby. Sugarbits refused to go any further, through. Animals have the sense for these kinds of things.

Ginny and Betsy hopped off. They thought Sugarbits might be a bit thirsty, so they led her to a nearby stream. She wouldn't drink.

"You know you can lead a horse to water, but you can't make to drink," Ginny stated.

"That's a good point, I gotta write that down."

They had a laugh, a much-needed one. There were a few whispers in the distance. It was time to explore and go where Sugarbits wouldn't. Ginny gave the horse a hug and they continued onward. Well, upward is more like it. They grabbed a hold of a few ledges and made their way up. They climbed a bit of the distance. They were both determined to get up as fast as they could. They climbed, and climbed, and climbed. The whispers grew louder as they went higher and higher.

"We gotta go quick, Ginny!" Betsy shouted. They were makin' good time, almost to the top. Betsy was almost ahead of Ginny.

"Slow down Betsy, it isn't sa...." Ginny pleaded.

Yup, Betsy had slipped as a few rocks had shaken loose. They were high up, and it was a long way down. Ginny jumped to her and reached down to grab her free hand. She grasped her hand close, and brought Betsy up as high as she could. Just then, the rocks above toppled onto her legs. Ginny pulled with all her might to keep her balance, but it was too late. She fell hundreds of feet below to the jagged rocks with Betsy.

Now, yer probably wonderin' what's happenin' in this story. But to tell you, we're gonna have to go back-a-ways. And it might sound a bit confusin', but up until this point, this had been what Ginny had remembered. But that's not how it all happened. You see, Ginny had lost her way when she was racin' to the camp to find Betsy. She never made it. The critters got a hold of her first.

Let's wind the sun back a few hours, and head to the camp. Boone came trekkin' through the forest, and saw Austin and Betsy cookin' over the fire. They looked pretty plain, just bidin' time.

"Where's Ginny?" Boone bellowed, out of breath.

"She was with you, you twit," Austin said. Boone looked straight to Betsy, who gave her a nod in agreement. It was *not* what he wanted to hear.

"She left me about an hour ago. She said she heard you scream and raced off down the cliff. I don't understand where she could have gone."

"Unless, of course, *they* got to her," Austin motioned out toward the cliffs where there were several animals perchin' and peerin' down.

"Not now, Austin," Betsy warned. She was worried he could be right. "I sure didn't scream, Boone."

"Are ya sure?"

"We haven't heard nothin' except for those pesky critters in the brush."

Well, we better stick to the mission. Let's gather some samples and get back to...." Austin began.

"Are you outta yer mind? We're not leavin' without Ginny!" Betsy said.

"Betsy, what's our plan, then?" Boone asked.

"We need to act heroic like Ginny. She wouldn't hesitate a moment if she thought one of us was in peril. Except maybe you, Austin."

"Right. Well, I don't like it, but I agree we should make an effort to find her, I guess. And when I rescue her, I'll be the best prospector in the West," Austin said as he gazed off into the distance.

Boone and Betsy just shook their heads. They thought that this man had never cared for anythin'. Now he did care for soemthin', and that was respect. But he sure as shoot hadn't earned it.

They gathered what was left of their gear, packed it onto Sugarbits, and made their way up the mountain, in search of a clue to lead them to Ginny. They did have a mission to do, so Boone ensured he collected samples of soil along the way. He conducted a few tests, all a part of the ruse. But with the crew on their way, it's best to pick up things with Ginny. If y'all happen to have a sensible brain in yer head, this may start to sound a bit screwy, and you'd be right, but it's how it happened.

Ginny woke up. She was tangled in all sorts of branches and vines. A nest of sorts. She was smack dab in the middle of Chick-A-Pin Hill, next to the natural spring flowin' right out of the mountain. She was dazed and confused.

"Who did this?! Show yer face!"

There was not a human soul 'round her, but there were plenty of animal souls that took notice of her awakenin'. They appeared to laugh at our hero. More and more animals surrounded her, and the more they did, the more she felt them in her heart. She no longer struggled in the tangle of shrubs.

There were birds, foxes, rabbits, and even bears comin' to observe. She peered around lookin' at them, straight into their eyes. She pondered again, *Was she daft? What was happenin'?*

That's when *it* happened.

At the same time Boone, Betsy, and Austin were makin' there way up the mountain, climbin' the rocks and passin' through the streams. Pleasant conversation had subsided, though.

Betsy tripped and fell on a jagged rock. She was bleedin' a bit.

"We couldn't possibly recommend this place as a site to mine," Boone stated frankly as he tended to Betsy's wound. Betsy was noticeable saddened by the reality. She grappled in her head with what the future would hold for her friends and family in Tumbleweed.

"Well, we're going to have to wait and see what the results say. It could be worth all the trouble. Once you blow a mountain open, it doesn't really matter," Austin said.

"Yer daft, there are not enough mechanics to make this here mountain safe. It would take years to excavate."

"Well, if it is too dangerous to mine, what will happen to Tumbleweed?" Betsy asked.

"Ginny will find a way. Everyone will move together if need be, just like Barnabas promised," Boone said.

Austin smirked. Boone, havin' a little courage, walked up to him and said, "Ginny has a way of makin' people keep their promises." Ginny would have been proud of her brother.

"You're right, Boone," Betsy said with a much-needed grin. She wiped her blood off in a stream and led the boys farther up toward the peak. As they climbed, they picked up the pace. There were a few animals peerin' from above. It felt like they were bein' watched.

Ginny was experiencin' somethin' that is simply too hard to describe. I'll do my best, of course. From her point of view, the cave began to change right in front of her. The animals morphed, from one animal to the next— one moment there'd be a bear, then it would change into a baby fox. Then, she blinked and saw that fox grow old. The animals surrounded her again and were transformin' in front of her.

"What is happenin'!"

The animals started to swarm her. Then all of a sudden they spread out, makin' room for a rabbit. It comforted her. She pet it and held it tight. The rabbit stood up on its legs and put its paw on her heart. Ginny got the message loud and clear.

Betsy and Boone had almost made it to the top of the mountain. They gathered themselves. Boone noticed somethin' was wrong. More like somethin' was missin'. Austin was nowhere to be found.

"Where is he?"

"I thought he was with you," Betsy said.

They called out for him, lookin' back down the mountain. They couldn't find nothin'. They came across a large waterfall barrelin' down the mountain. They could see animals comin' and goin' right at the spout.

"We need to get in there," Betsy said.

Boone nodded and attempted to climb up.

"Look over there!" Betsy screamed. She pointed at a bunch of little critters headin' around the mountainside. They raced 'round, followin' the critters. Austin's pack was tossed aside, and they could see his trail. It led straight to a small hole. Boone got down on all fours and took a look.

"Wow, it opens up just a few feet into a big cave. We've gotta break though."

"It's impossibly small," Betsy said.

"You leave that to me."

Boone took out a doodad and jammed it into the little hole.

"This is an explosive. It won't cause much damage, just enough for us to fit through."

Boone lit the fuse and grabbed Betsy to take cover.

BOOM!

Ginny stood there holdin' that rabbit. She wouldn't know how to explain it, but she knew in her heart that if the mountain were to be mined it would destroy all animal life for hundreds of miles. Animals depended on it. The rabbit slowly slipped away, leavin' her there. The other animals left, too. She sat still, thinkin' in her head. She knew in her heart that she had to protect this mountain. No matter how. The animals needed her protectin'. They had done what they could up until that point to tell her. Ginny knew that those stories about the mountain, with all those disappearin' pioneers, must've been true. Alone, she sat in deep thought.

Boone cleared away the debris from the rocks that had caved in. The explosion caused a bit of a mess. Nothin' they couldn't clean up. The hole was now a few feet wide. Betsy was excited and hurried in.

"Wait!" Boone screamed.

The hole wasn't big enough. Betsy knocked a few rocks loose, causing her to be stuck. Boone feverishly threw rocks out of the way, attemptin' to free her. The rocks seemed to keep pilin' up the more Boone kept diggin'. When all luck was lost ,Betsy started to laugh.

"The animals! They're lickin' me," she chucked.

At first it was fine, but then it became torturous. I'm sure y'all have experienced that type of thing before. She pleaded with Boone to help her escape. The animals continued to lick. Just tellin' you gives me the heeby-jeebies.

Ginny sat in what could only be described as a trance. She was thinkin' about everythin' she had seen that day, and everythin' she had experienced in her life. All the loved ones she had let go, and all the loved ones she hadn't loved enough. Her mind was a storm of regrets. She recalled back to when she was a kid. She regretted the chances she didn't take, and the times she didn't stand tall. This moment changed her. She was stronger. The animals had made her stronger.

The animals had stopped lickin' Betsy, and Boone had broken through the rocks into the cave inside of Chick-A-Pin Hill. The critters scurried away. Boone felt close as they raced inside the mountain. There were waterfalls and streams everywhere. They were close to the natural springs. They heard a moan up ahead. They saw Austin strung up in a thread of vines.

"Austin!" Betsy yelled.

Austin seemed shaken, but awoke from his knocked-out state. Boone and Betsy rushed to help. Just then, a vicious bear and fox leapt from behind a pile of rocks. They slowly crept toward Boone and Betsy. Betsy grabbed Boone by the arm.

The bear leapt onto Boone and pinned him to the ground. He was completely covered by the bear and could've been crushed at any moment. Betsy took out Austin's pistol from her bag and aimed the gun at the bear.

"Wait!" Austin screamed.

There stood Ginny. She felt the presence of Boone, Betsy, and Austin, and motioned them over. The bear that had pinned Boone licked his face all over, showerin' him in spit. It made him laugh, as he gently stood up. Boone took out a knife and slashed Austin free. Austin was shaken but managed to take a few steps towards Ginny.

Ginny gave Betsy a big hug and shared the journey she'd been on.

"These animals have spoken to me. They will grant us safe passage home, but we must never come back again. We mustn't tell anyone what we saw neither."

"The animals? They spoke to you?" Austin doubtfully asked. The moment he spoke, the animals around him grew angry and snarled. The once-friendly bear roared.

"Fine, okay, we'll leave and never return," Austin said.

"I don't believe this. I am seein' it, but I don't believe it!" Boone said.

"This defies explanation," Betsy added.

"This is what they have told me. I felt it in my heart, and the heart is the most important thing to trust," Ginny continued.

The rabbit hopped toward Ginny and leapt into her hand. She gave it a cozy hug.

"We will leave at once. Can you help us get out of here?" Ginny said.

"This is ridiculous," Austin said.

The rabbit hopped down and joined the other animals in leadin' the group. They passed through the caverns, passed a whole patch of briar that looked like it would be quite painful to touch, and made it to the natural springs. There was plenty of water gushin' down, creatin' a waterfall leavin' the cave. It was the peak of Chick-A-Pin Hill. Ginny couldn't muster any words. She simply reached out to pet the friendly wildlife and especially that rabbit. As she stood up from pettin' the critters, a blue bird flew in from the outside and perched on her shoulder.

"How beautiful," Betsy said.

Boone took a closer look, admirin' its beauty.

"It's time to go now," Ginny said.

"How?" Austin asked.

Ginny motioned to the rushin' waterfall that was barrelin' down the side of the mountain.

"You're daft!" Austin said.

Betsy and Boone linked arms with Ginny and they jumped into the water and waded toward the edge.

"Suit yourself!" Boone shouted through the waves.

Austin took one long look at the animals who were growin' angry at his presence. He slowly walked over to the water's edge. That ol' bear roared. Austin lost his footin' and fell into the water with a big ol' splash! He floated closer to the waterfall, and grabbed hold of Ginny.

"1...2...3!"

They plummeted down that mountain, splashin' down below.

"*YEEHAAW!*" Ginny shouted. She enjoyed that part.

They floated over to the edge of the river and gathered their stuff. Ginny whistled loudly for Sugarbits, who promptly trotted out from around the corner.

"It's time to head back," Ginny said as she hopped onto the saddle. The group promptly followed Betsy's lead toward the frontier forest. They could see a bit of a glow in the distance. It was their humble town of Tumbleweed. Ginny knew she had to have a plan.

"Nobody will ever believe us about what happened. We'd all be locked in the looney bin if we were to tell," Ginny said. "I lived it and I don't even know if I believe it."

"You know there's tons of gold to be mined from there. You would be rich beyond your wildest dreams," Austin countered.

"I made a promise to those animals that we'd never return and that we'd do what we could to ensure nobody else did, either. They could have killed us, and they'd probably kill anybody who ever comes back."

"Nonsense. We could blast those animals before they knew what hit them. Tell her, Boone."

"He's right, but he's not *right*," Boone replied.

"We need to dump out the soil. Do it, Boone," Betsy said.

Boone promptly dumped his different soil samples into a nearby stream and grabbed some other samples that would be used as decoys.

"You're making a big mistake," Austin said.

Ginny walked up to Austin. "We need you to go along with this story, Austin. We are countin' on you. If this gets out of hand, everyone we know could be hurt. That's goin' to all be on you, and for what? Gold? Power? Gold may make you wealthy, but it will never be enough. There will always be somethin' more. You need to get rich in other ways. By helpin' and contributin' to the greater good."

"Spare me the speech. I'll go along with your little plan, but one day I am going to need something from you, and I am not going to ask twice," Austin said.

"You have my word," Ginny said.

They shook hands in agreement, and headed toward town. It was late now, almost time for the midnight revue at the Gold Dust Saloon.

"Let's regroup at dawn we can all meet Barnabas together," Austin said.

"No. We need to go now, no use waitin' for the mornin'," Ginny said, "Let's go."

Barnabas had rather lavish livin' quarters close to the Big Thunder Mine Operation. He liked to be near his investment. They walked up to his door and gave it a poundin'.

Barnabas opened the door, appearin' to have just awoken.

"Thank's for coming. Welcome back. I want a full report! Come sit down."

They sat in his parlor room. Up on the wall were several painted portraits of himself in heroic poses. He'd never been to any of the places depicted, of course. Barnabas took notice of Betsy.

"And what's she doing here?"

"Well, I needed an extra member on the crew. Luckily, she agreed," Ginny said with a wink.

"Okay, never mind, let's hear it."

"Well, it was quite an interestin' thing, really. We went up and down that mountain. It was rather dangerous. Really, dark too. And you wouldn't believe it! There were tons of ruthless animals. We managed to gather samples, of course. Boone, can you tell us the results?"

"Sure, of course," Boone said as he placed various glasses of samples on the table.

"Test one, here, we gathered at the base. We found absolutely no traces of gold or silver."

"Test two, we gathered on the way up to the top, nothin'. Test three contains soil from the heart of the mountain. We had blasted into a cave of sorts, nothin'. We then went even further with this sample." He pointed to the fourth test glass.

"I get it. You found nothin'," Barnabas said with disappointment. Ginny gave Austin a look. She wanted him to chime in and validate.

"Yup, nothin'," Austin added.

"This is quite a disappointment. What will happen to this humble town? What will happen to all those poor people who depend on me for jobs?" Barnabas asked, pretendin' to be sincere.

"It's a shame'," Boone said.

"Okay, then, it looks like our business here is done. I'll show you to the door. Austin, please stay behind. Let's talk a bit of business so I can catch you up for tomorrow. Lots of things to do now."

Ginny, Betsy, and Boone went to the Gold Dust Saloon for a night cap. It had been a heck of a day, one of the wildest days they'd ever had in the wilderness. They took their seat at Ginny's table. The workers took notice of Betsy's messed-up look. She'd rarely been seen covered in mud.

"That's a nice look you got on, Betsy. I think I like it better than your stage look," Ginny said with a smile.

"Does this mean I get to be your sidekick and go on all your adventures with ya?"

"We'll see, we'll see."

They shared a few laughs and a few secrets and felt closer than ever before. Boone had gained a little courage, Betsy had been on a true adventure, and Ginny had saved the animals of Chick-A-Pin Hill.

Meanwhile, Austin and Barnabas had unfinished business.

"So, Austin, what did you really find out there at Chick-A-Pin Hill?" Barnabas asked.

Austin took out a sack of dirt from his pack and threw it on the table. A bit poured out and there were specks of gold and silver shimmerin'.

"Enough to triple your net worth."

Wickedly Ever After

a Fantasyland short story by Kristen Waldbieser

Through the mist, through the woods, through the darkness and the shadows, a small tavern could be seen peeking through the trees. Dirty, dusty, and dreary, the old establishment looked like it could fall over at any minute. However, the sounds of clanging cups, clashing swords, and familiar pub songs brought life to such a dark place. Outside, a large sign sat above the door with just a few simple words. The name, Gaston's Tavern, hung proudly with its bright gold print. Oh, yes, reader, the very Gaston that you know and love.

Inside, he sat in a large chair, antlers surrounding him from every angle. He drank his Lafou's Brew, the only thing in the tavern named after his trusty sidekick instead of himself. He swayed back and forth as the ruffians and thugs sang sad songs of their terrible defeats. Be thankful, reader, that you were not actually there for the event. Your ears will be forever grateful.

Next to him sat the most evil villains that the sweet little kingdom of Fantasyland had ever seen. Captain James Hook leaned against the fireplace, his eyes following the clock that sat on its' edge. Next to him sat Vanessa. After the incident with that little mermaid, a sea-witch once called Ursula vowed she would never use the name or aquatic form ever again. Next to her, Her Majesty sat, the most evil of them all, the Wicked Queen that almost poisoned the fairest in the land. She sat reading her books of spells, stirring her drink without even touching it.

No one said a word. They gazed off in to the crowd of thugs. This is how their evenings were usually spent, remembering the days that they would spread terror and fear throughout the land. The days that they ruled, and weren't shunned to a small neighboring village.

The pirates and thugs sang, and sang, and sang. Their brews sloshed to the floor, their voices getting louder and louder. And unfortunately, louder does not always mean better. The thugs had taken the floor, singing about their dreams that never came true.

Vanessa pushed back from the table and stood up. She walked over to one of the thugs.

"Would you *stop?* Day after day, I tell you to stop singing the same old songs. Now today, I mean it. Stop before I take your voice away, too," she hissed in his ear, pointing to one of the thugs that looked back at her, terror in his eyes. He didn't say a word.

"Sit down, Vanessa. It's not right for a woman to be acting like that," Gaston said. Her Majesty glared at him. To this day, I will never find the right words to describe that glare.

"I quite agree," Her Majesty began. Gaston's smug grin spread across his face.

"With Vanessa," she continued. Gaston crossed his arms and slumped down in his chair.

"We've been stuck out here for too long. This tiny little tavern is the only place for us. And now, *a year* has gone by since they put up their perfect little barrier," Vanessa said, walking toward the window. Hook looked after her.

Oh, do you have a question, reader? Of course, what is the barrier? Exactly one year ago, to the day, the villains found themselves banished from the kingdom of Fantasyland. The fairy godmothers had developed a spell so powerful, that no amount of evil would ever be able to break through it. It would forevermore separate all good from evil. From that day on, there would be no more battles, no more evil spells, just the *good* ones finally living their ultimate happily ever after.

Yawn.

"Haven't we tried before? We've tried the usual spells, battles, everything. Those little royals have their pixie dust and magic wands that beat us every time," Hook said.

It was a question I had pondered for years, and perhaps that's why I took such an interest in this wicked bunch. How could the most powerful villains in the world, backed by magic spells and evil henchmen, always get beaten by fairies? It never quite made sense, but none of the villains ever really wanted to talk about it. Too soon, I suppose.

"Well, then, we try something else! There has to be one spell in that book that we haven't used on those perfect little princes and princesses," Vanessa said. She walked over to the window on the far side of the tavern, perfectly positioned to see into the magnificent kingdom.

Through the window, they saw visions of princes twirling their princesses, and fairy godmothers practicing their latest dress transformations. Joyful music could be heard, though faintly, bringing words of love and happiness. All that nonsense that they'd heard over and over again. They were all beautiful, and seamed to be glowing in the pixie dust that the villains hated so much. Beautiful sounds filled the air and clashed with the harsh harmonies that the pirates were now singing. Vanessa watched as a handsome Prince Eric twirled his beloved little mermaid, who was dancing around on her legs.

"Ungrateful princess. I give her exactly what she wanted, and how did she repay me?!" Vanessa did have a point, after all. The mermaid got the prince and the happily ever after that went along with it.

"Get away from there. You always end up complaining for hours after you stand there watching," Hook said as he sat down in the chair next to him. It had turned into their nightly routine. Cursing the days of the past and watching out the window toward a world they could no longer enter.

But, what were they going to do about it? You know the stories—they lost. They were banished to the far side of the kingdom, the part that the royals had forgotten about, hidden behind a dark forest that the Evil Queen had banished a certain princess to long ago. It was a bit of a cruel irony, really. A land where they would never find their own happily ever afters. Good would never defeat evil, it would always triumph, blah, blah, blah. This writer, however, was not buying it.

I moved over to the far side of the room and pushed a crying hooligan off the piano bench. The piano stopped, but it did not prevent the ruffians from going on, and on, and on. I stretched my fingers out over the keys and began to play.

Do me do so do so mi do...

At first, no one noticed the switch to the melodious tune. They continued to sing over my music, but one by one, they began to stop. Soon, the entire tavern was staring at me, pure silence. I continued on, making the notes brighter and stronger. Finally, someone broke the silence.

"What is that *noise?!*" Vanessa shrieked. I didn't answer her, I continued to play. I watched as the villainous four began to inch their way toward me. Soon, they were surrounding the piano I had claimed as my own. The captain slammed his hook onto the keys.

"Tell me, my dear, just what do you think you are doing?" he said as he raised his hook toward my nose. I slowly stopped playing and stared him straight in the eyes.

"Helping you finally win," I answered.

Ah yes, reader. It's interesting to think that a simple narrator in a story has a part to play as well, don't you agree? Because, let's face it, sometimes the characters in the story need a little push. Even if they won't be the ones to admit it.

"We don't need your help. No one plots like Gaston!" Gaston said. Yes, he really would talk in third person.

"But if we did inquire about your idea – what did you have in mind?" Her Majesty asked.

I didn't respond, I just continued to play the simple little tune louder and louder and louder. They all looked at each other. Surely, one of them would catch on soon.

They all stared at me. I raised my eyebrows at them as I played a little faster, making each note stand out from the one before.

"You could try...." I began.

"Throwing a piano at the castle!" Gaston said proudly. A true genius.

"Not exactly what I had in mind." They continued to think.

"Fill their land with the music my pirates sing all day? I'm sure that would be quite a change for them!" Hook added. Now they were getting somewhere.

"A fantastic idea. But isn't that so...typical? They could stop that before you even began."

"Then what exactly are you thinking of?" Her Majesty asked. They all stood staring at each other, completely dumbfounded about the idea. I tell you, I've never seen a look of complete disbelief as I did in that moment.

"Perhaps think of a different song...." I hinted. They all nodded, acting as if it had been their idea from the very beginning.

"I've got one! *You'll love the life of a thief, you'll relish....*"

"Absolutely not! *No one sings like Gast....*"

"Enough of that! *You poor unfortunate....*"

"I said try something *different*," I interrupted.

"I know!" Her Majesty yelled, her voice completely filling the room. Every ruffian, pirate, thug, and witch froze in complete terror. "What did we just discuss? We know the results of our music. We need one of these little tunes filled with peace, love, and harmony." Quickly, the villains all began to laugh.

"Peace?! Love?! And what do we know about any of that?" Gaston asked, laughing.

Her Majesty said with a dark laugh, "We don't. And that's what will make it so perfectly wicked. We'll create a new song, one that will be beloved by all. It will be such a spell, the type of song they will never be able to forget, no matter how hard they try. The tune will remain in their ears forever, and though it's merry they will never hear another song ever again."

Let me tell you, reader. These villains clearly did not know anything about peace or love. The songs always ended the same way—revealing some key point in their wicked plot. But isn't that the way it always goes?

"What is it that Peter Pan is always...."

"*Don't* say that name," Hook warned. I paused.

"Apologies, Captain. But for once, you have to listen. Think of the happiest things." The villains all shuddered at the sound of it. However, their scowls softened, and they realized that I had made quite an excellent point.

Her Majesty approached me quickly. "How do we trust you? What are your motives behind all this?" she asked, staring a cold, harsh stare straight into my eyes. If looks could kill, well, I'm not sure I would be here to tell you the tale.

However, I suppose you must have been wondering this question yourself, haven't you? For the first time, your train of thought might be right alongside the most wicked of them all.

Let that settle in your brain for a moment.

All right, I won't keep you in suspense for much longer. Let's all face it. There is nothing worse than a story with no excitement. There is nothing worse than a perfect, storybook world with no conflict. And, as someone who had grown up in a perfect, storybook world, this writer was ready to bring back that excitement.

I know, I know. How could I possibly unleash the most evil of them all onto sweet princes and princesses, guiding them every step of the way? Well, let's look at the track record so far. How do you *really* think the story will play out?

I said,"I'm on this side of the barrier, just as much as you are. Doesn't that show where my loyalties lie?" Her Majesty raised her eyebrows and I almost saw the hint of a smile spread across her face.

"You're one of us, now," Vanessa said to me. I nodded. The moment was brief, and I'm not really sure who it was for. Perhaps their own peace of mind, believing that maybe, just maybe, someone outside their usual group of sidekicks was on their side.

"I've done it!" Hook announced, showing a piece of paper that was attached to his hook. He had been working on the lyrics, the happiest of them all. With his elegant diction, everyone agreed he would be best fit for the job. The group huddled around the table, reading over the most lovely lyrics they had ever heard.

Soon after, Vanessa finished creating the melody, singing it to the group. Slowly, she made her way through every line. The words were joyful, but the music, well, was a bit sad.

"It needs something," Gaston said. He looked in pain as he thought of what it could be.

"Certainly not a change in the lyrics! They're perfect!" Hook argued.

"No, but something just isn't right," Her Majesty said.

Apparently, I would have to intervene again. "Maybe...it's a little slow? Try making it a bit more up tempo." They all quickly nodded, and Vanessa sang again. This time, much faster.

The music echoed through the little tavern. Its happy tune perfectly matched with the lyrics of peace and love. The pirates and thugs around the tavern all groaned, as if in pain, at the sound of it. We all agreed that the song was complete.

Vanessa sang the song into a beautiful shell that she had turned into a necklace. The queen dipped the necklace in her cauldron, enchanting it. Gaston watched, critiquing every step along the way.

"It's absolutely brilliant!"

"Nothing like it before!"

"Incredible!"

And then they all stood there. Staring at each other, completely unsure of their next move. Remember, reader, these used to be the most fearsome villains throughout any kingdom. But, as the years passed and the stories faded, so did their confidence. After losing battle after battle after battle, you begin to question if you really were ever fearsome at all.

"We'll play the song over and over and over again, until it's really the only thing they can think about!" Vanessa began.

"They'll look for an escape, a way to once again serenade their sweethearts with the song they fell in love with, as we know they will," Her Majesty added.

"That's when you," Gaston pointed to me, "will trick them into lifting the barrier, so that they may escape to a land where they will no longer hear the song." They all nodded. I went along with it.

"Who's to say they'll even dislike the song?" Hook asked.

Her Majesty ignited her eyes once more. "Thanks to my enchantment, the song will continue to go on and on and on, until it is all that they can hear. No matter how joyous we have made it—the shear repetitive nature of it will ensure they run." No one wanted to question her after that. Would you?

There was much more discussion, of course. When would they do this? How would one of them get through the barrier? All very legitimate questions. However, most of the conversation fell on who would take the credit for the plan.

"I've said it before, I'll say it again! No one plots like Gaston. Clearly, this is my clever plan," Gaston said.

"These are the kinds of things that I *live* for. And without my melodious tune, there would be no spell to begin with," Vanessa argued.

"And am I not the one providing these happy little thoughts? We would be nowhere without me!" Hook said.

Her Majesty did not even need an explantation. Although all of the villains were wicked, they all feared the most evil of them all.

After much deliberation, and perhaps a little prodding from one impatient writer, they put their pettiness aside, focusing on the problem ahead of them. How to get past the barrier.

The barrier ran all the way across the kingdom; there was no way around it, that was guaranteed. Had they tried before? Of course! Countless hours of trying different spells, disguises, you name it. But they had never prevailed. So what would make this time any different? Well, you'll just have to wait and see.

"We should sail along the kingdom, sneaking around the north side," Hook suggested.

"And in what? Your inconspicuous pirate ship?" Vanessa asked.

Gaston looked puzzled.

"Well, what do you suggest? We waltz right up to the barrier?" Hook asked.

A waltz, so beautiful, simple, and pure. You know all of the classic stories. Cinderella met her Prince Charming waltzing the night away, the Beast even whisked Belle off her feet during their magnificent dance. And maybe, just maybe, it would be enough to sneak their precious gift through.

It certainly wouldn't be easy. One of the barrier's greatest powers was its invisibility. The villains always thought that was the most wicked part of it all, allowing them to see the world that they had been banished from. However, this made battling the barrier even more difficult. Any sight of a villain would send any princess screaming for help, and the entire plan would be ruined. No, this time, they had to be clever, and outsmart the obstacles that laid before them.

"We can't just walk up to the center of the kingdom. We'll be spotted for sure," Gaston said. He had just caught up with the rest of the plan.

"No, I do think Hook is right about approaching by the side," Her Majesty said. Hook was beaming. It took a lot for Her Majesty to say any sort of agreement or compliment.

"And you don't think those prim little princesses will see his ship?!" Vanessa squeaked.

"Did I say take his boat? No, we'll sail along the north side in an unrecognizable boat. Hook, I'm sure one of your men has something we could use?"

"Aye, they do."

"As we approach, you will play the role of a wary princess, visiting from a far-away kingdom," Her Majesty said pointing to me. "Gaston, you'll have to accompany her, but you will need to disguise yourself if this is to work."

"As a tree!" Gaston blurted out. Everyone stared at him.

"As a *prince*," Vanessa said, rolling her eyes.

I hadn't quite expected to be a big part of the plot, really. More just watching the story unfold or giving some small assistance. But, there was no turning back now. I had to finish what I had started, or you, my dear reader, would have nothing to read beyond these words.

Hook didn't bother asking a member of his crew if he could use his boat. He just led us to the docks, where an assortment of ships, the *Jolly Rodger* being the grandest of them all, were waiting. Right next to it sat a small boat. Well, I'm not quite sure you could call it a boat, as it looked like it was about to sink to the bottom of the sea.

"You expect me to sail in that? But there are so many other ships to choose from," Gaston said. Clearly, he still hadn't understood what the word *inconspicuous* meant.

"This will do," Her Majesty said. That was all that needed to be said, and we boarded the *Upstream Plunge*, a horrific name for a boat if you ask me.

Unfortunately, Hook realized that his new crew was not quite used to sea life. Gaston stood at the wheel, convinced that this was the perfect angle for him. Her Majesty stood at the front, simply looking out ahead of them. Vanessa, who was used to being *under* the boats, pretended to know exactly what she was doing as she untied the boat from the dock. As for me, I had read many books on pirates and sea voyages, and they always explained how to navigate the waters. I could at least pretend I knew what I was doing and play the role of first mate.

It wasn't a long journey, just around the riverbend. Soon, we approached the side of the kingdom, and you could see the faint silhouette of a castle, just peeking over the trees. It was a magnificent sight, just as it was the first time I had seen it.

"Fairies!" Vanessa whispered to the rest of us, as if the fairy godmothers on the far dock could hear her. It meant we were getting close, and the most difficult part of our plan would soon begin.

After prying the wheel away from Gaston, who really had no business being there in the first place, Hook maneuvered the boat behind a group of trees. The first, admittedly the easiest, phase of the plan was complete. Get to the docks.

With nothing more than the wave of her hand, Her Majesty transformed the simple dress I was wearing into a beautiful ballgown, fit for any princess.

"Disgustingly beautiful," Her Majesty said as she created it.

Following that, she transformed Gaston's hunting attire into a suit that any prince would be envious of. Everyone was impressed. No one had ever expected her to use such *good* magic before. She may have even impressed herself.

"It won't last long. Magic doesn't last forever. So do your job. Quickly!" Her Majesty warned. I wasn't about to question her.

"You know what to do," Vanessa said to me, handing me a beautifully decorated box. It looked as if a fairy godmother had created it, perfectly concealing the necklace safely hidden inside.

"Wait! It needs one more thing," Hook said. He approached me with a small sack that had a shining, shimmering, splendid glow all around it.

"How did you get your hands on pixie dust?" Vanessa screeched. She watched as it glistened against the sunlight.

"What? You think I let that little Tinker go without collecting a bit of dust as she flew off? I've been saving it for a moment just like this."

What was so important about the pixie dust, you may ask? Well, think about it. A magical barrier designed to ward off all evil wouldn't exactly take kindly to a gift given by the Wicked Queen herself. However, coating the gift in the purest and, well, *good* thing in all the land just might be wicked enough to work.

"Now, you all hide, below deck," Gaston ordered, even though the rest of our crew was already heading down the stairs.

The two of us stood at the wheel, and I held my breath. Slowly, we approached a dock that was filled with fairy godmothers practicing magic spells, and mermaids splashing in the lagoon. For a moment, it was peaceful.

"Ahoy! Ahoy, there!" Gaston shouted.

We sailed the boat right next to the dock, and Gaston dropped the anchor. He held out his hand, helping me off the boat.

"Hello, my dears. And who, might I ask, are you?" One of the fairy godmothers, named Rosebud, asked.

"Oh, we seem to have gotten lost! We had taken a journey, and, well, we may have gotten a little carried away. Do you mind if my kind prince checks our boat for any damages? We hit some rocks a ways back, and just want to make sure it is okay," I said, holding my breath with every word. The fairy godmothers smiled.

"Of course you may. But, you still have not answered my question as to who you are," she said, a little less patient this time.

"Haven't I? Oh, it has been such a long night!" I giggled. The fairy was joined by another, named Lilly, who had suddenly gained interest in our conversation. *Think, think, think!*

"Princess Emalina," I said convincingly, "And that would be Prince...."

"I am Prince Gast...Gastoffinus!" Gaston shouted from the boat. Another shining moment for this clever *prince*.

"Princess Emalina, it is a pleasure to meet you. Although I must say that I have never heard of you or your prince before. What kingdom are you from?" Lilly asked.

"It is the kingdom of...pure...enchantment—though nothing can compare to the enchanting beauty of my love," Gaston interjected, jumping from the boat to the dock next to me. For a brute, he could be quite charming.

"Excuse me, my lovely fairies, but this music is so enticing, I must ask that I share a dance with my fair Princess Emalina," he added, bowing to the fairies. Even now, they were blushing.

"Well, we could never say no to such a pure and true love!" another fairy godmother, named Daisy, squealed.

They stepped aside as Gaston scooped me up into his arms, and spun me around and around. With every twist and twirl, we watched, waiting for the moment when the fairy godmothers would look away. We smiled, giggled, and moved delicately to the music. I had never been one for dancing, but our dance could not stop until just the right moment.

"First, finish the dance. Make them love us, then you know what to do!" Gaston whispered to me. I knew the plan, but the reminder kept me focused.

We ended our dance with a bow and a curtsy. The fairy godmothers, who had now turned their attention toward us, applauded.

"Oh, that was lovely. Now, you must join us for an afternoon tea, don't you think? Lilly makes the most delightful biscuits in the entire kingdom!" Rosebud said.

"That sounds wonderful. However, we have already been away from home for far too long. And it looks as if the rocks did not damage our ship too much, so we should be fine to sail the rest of the way. But we thank you for such kind, although brief, hospitality," Gaston said. I was shocked. Hospitality was a big word for him.

"Understandable. But remember, you are always welcome back in our kingdom!" Lilly said. Gaston nodded toward me. It was time.

"You know, you have been so kind to us. Welcoming us into your kingdom, even if just for a brief moment. Darling, would you please go on the boat and retrieve a token of gratitude for our new friends?" I said to Gaston. He smiled, running back to the boat.

"Oh, you mustn't! Really, we are always happy to help traveling royals," one of the fairy godmothers said. I couldn't tell you which one; I had all of their floral names confused at this point. Luckily, I didn't have to think about it long before Gaston was back with the sparkling box.

"Please, it isn't much, but our kingdom is a small and happy place. And we would like to share this bit of happiness with you," I said, handing the box to Rose, who gladly took it.

"That really is too kind. Is this pixie dust?" Daisy asked, examining the box.

"It is! We have a small group of fairies who have made our land their home, and those little tinkers are always looking for ways to enhance the kingdom. Lately, they've taken to using it to create small tokens of gratitude. They'll be so pleased to hear that it was given!" I said. The fairy godmothers were all smiling from ear to ear.

After more pleasantries, back and forths of "thank you," "you really shouldn't have," and "you're just too kind," it was time to say goodbye. We thanked them once more and boarded the ship. Before sailing away, we watched as the three fairy godmothers turned around and walked toward the barrier. Would it actually work?

They walked right through. Holding our little box, they walked right through.

And now, the next stage of our plan could begin.

We set sail, ensuring that our boat turned a sharp corner to be hidden behind a large bush along the shore. Before long, the rest of our crew burst out of the deck below.

"Did you do it?! Is it there?" Vanessa asked. I nodded, unsure of what all I should say.

"Your Majesty, I believe it is time," Hook added. The Evil Queen nodded, and opened her spell book.

Chanting an incantation, one that I would never be able to pen down, even if I tried, Her Majesty began her wicked work. Her voice was monotone, strong, but most of all, powerful. She finished her spell, closed her book, and we all waited. It seemed like an eternity had passed.

"Shouldn't it be doing something by now?" Gaston asked. Everyone looked at each other. It should have started something. Even a hum of a tune. Perhaps the plan wasn't going to work after all....

"Try chanting that spell again!" Vanessa demanded. Her Majesty eyed her down. Both powerful queens of magic, neither one would ever back down to the other. Without saying another word, Her Majesty began to cast her spell again.

Still nothing.

"If I had to pretend to be a royal for *nothing*...." Gaston began.

"It won't be for nothing. We might just have to change our strategy," Hook said. You could actually see the cogs moving in his mind. "It seems to me that your spell, however powerful, is being blocked by the barrier. Why we didn't think of this before is beyond me." It was honestly the most clever thing I had heard from the bunch this entire time. Even I hadn't thought of that.

"Are you telling me we're *stuck*?!" Vanessa screeched. It did seem like it.

"No. I'm saying someone needs to cast the spell from the other side of the barrier," Hook said, as if it were no issue at all.

"Oh, sure! Let's just walk right on through!" Gaston mocked. Suddenly, I felt Her Majesty's cold stare on me. Oh, no.

"Perhaps...." She began. I already knew where this was going.

"I'm not good or evil. I'm just a writer. Perhaps I can go through," I finished for her. She nodded. The rest of the group agreed. It was the only way to make the plan work.

Before I could bat an eye, I was facing the kingdom yet again, exiting the *Upstream Plunge*. I was still hidden behind large trees, invisible to any fairy godmothers or princesses. For now. I could hear the whispers of my crew behind me, pointing ahead of me, as if I could not see the shimmering barrier. I clutched Her Majesty's spell book in my hands as I walked forward.

I could tell that the bushes and trees were growing smaller and smaller as I continued on. I could begin to see the tops of tiaras and wings, and I knew my hiding place wouldn't last much longer. I just had to step through the barrier, chant the spell, and get out. That was it.

Behind me, I could still see the four waving at me, making large hand gestures to point me in the direction they wanted me to go. Move. Faster. Go. Straight.

I could see a pair of wings flying closer to me, growing larger as they approached the hedge I was hiding behind. Don't get caught. That was my only instruction. I hit the ground, crawling straight in to the greenery next to me. I stared through the leaves until the wings would disappear. Five seconds, ten, twenty...twenty-eight seconds. Then they were gone.

I crawled out of the hedge, thankfully to see no one around me. I ran as fast as I could in these ridiculous heels and petticoats.

Finally, I found myself face to face with the barrier that the villains feared so much. I only had once chance to do this. If I didn't, it was all over. I held my breath and stepped forward.

I made it through.

The book, however, did not.

It was still in my hand, yes. But I could not pull it through the barrier that was behind me. I pulled and pulled, but nothing seemed to work. Those fairy godmothers were better at this than I had thought. I panicked for a moment, and kept trying to pull it through. No matter what I did, I couldn't.

I sighed, finally thinking clearly, and stuck my other hand through the barrier, opening the book, which I now held in both hands. I flipped through the pages to the spell that Her Majesty had marked for me. A spell that she had taught Vanessa so many years ago. Now I just had to say the spell. Quickly, strongly, *powerfully*.

"Beluga, servuga, come winds of the Caspian Sea. Larnex, glossitis, et max larynxitis la voce to me," I chanted.

After a few moments, I began to hear it. The purest song that they had ever heard, filled with the happiest thoughts in all of the kingdom. It played, at first quietly, but I could gradually hear it more and more, until the lyrics were clear as a bell.

It's a world of laughter, a world of tears....

I ran back to the *Upstream Plunge,* finally releasing my breath for what seemed like the first time all day. My counterparts cheered as I approached. We could hear the song from the boat now. It had worked.

We all returned to the tavern, the villains pouring draughts of their favorite, LeFou's Brew. They laughed, cheering to their successes while clanking their glasses together.

"Don't celebrate so soon. Our work is not over yet," I warned. Oh, you know the stories. The villain thinks they have everything tied up, the battle is over, they've won. When really, you're only twenty minutes into the story, and the hero has started their own plan. It's a pitfall so common that they would fall into the trap time after time after time.

"Oh, enough! We've made it this far. There's no way we can be stopped now!" Gaston shouted, thumping his boots on the table in front of him.

It *did* seem to be that way. As I replayed the plot in my head, there didn't seem to be as many holes as there usually were in a villainous plan. There couldn't be a way that we could actually win this, could there? No, it was impossible. I walked over to the window and stared at the kingdom in the distance.

As for this next bit, I may have had a source on the inside of the kingdom telling me exactly what had happened....

The song spread throughout the kingdom, reaching far past the docks. A beautiful red-headed princess danced in the center of the town with her dashing prince, singing songs of their love and adventures. Quickly, their own song was drowned out by the new lyrics that were filling the land.

It's a world of hopes and a world of fears....

"Oh, how wonderful! The fairy godmothers must be trying to create some new songs for us. It's so nice to dance to," Princess Ariel said. Prince Eric spun her around, dancing to the new music.

Nearby, other happy couples acknowledged the new song. Snow White twirled around and around with her handsome prince, and Belle and her prince even took a moment from their books to listen to it. There are even rumors that Peter Pan began to dance with Wendy Darling, an activity that he would normally never do. They danced, danced, and danced, laughing and singing along to the song.

Princess Ariel ran over to a group of young fairy godmothers in training, who were listening closely to the song as well.

"The new music is such a refreshing change! Whoever wrote this song, well done! We absolutely love it," she said to the group. At first the godmothers hesitated, looking to each other for the answer. Finally, it was the young godmother named Rose who spoke up.

"We're so glad you like it! It was time for a change, wasn't it?" The other godmothers played along, nodding and smiling.

"You're all so incredible! You know how to make this kingdom the happiest place on earth!"

"Just as it always will be!" the fairy godmother Lily said.

It's a small world after all....

"Are you sure they won't just love it, and actually *want* to hear it over and over again?" Captain Hook asked, pulling me out of my trance from the window.

"Anything, no matter how good it is, would be annoying after so many times, " Vanessa said. It was true. The song was lovely, but just wait until it had played over and over and over again. But perhaps the spell wouldn't work. It wouldn't be the first time their foolproof plan fell through, right?

"Should we make it louder? Move things along a bit quicker?" Vanessa asked, clearly impatient with all of this waiting around.

"Unnecessary. All good things to those who wait," Her Majesty said.

And they did. Tick tock, tick tock, they waited. They all sat, listening to the thugs and pirates, just as they had before. It was almost like nothing had happened, and we were back at the beginning of the story. However, now the silence of these fearsome four was not filled with boredom and exasperation, but with tension and anticipation. I returned to the window, watching the outside world play on.

It had been four hours gone now, with nothing but those words playing over and over again. The princesses, one by one, had stopped dancing. Belle had returned to her book, Peter Pan was dashing around as he had before. The smiles remained on their faces, but a twinge of something more gleamed in their eyes. It was the fairest of them all that finally spoke.

"I do think this song is lovely, but I was wondering if there might be a different tune that I might whistle along to?" she asked a young fairy godmother named Daisy.

There's so much that we share that it's time we're aware
It's a small world after all.

"Oh, we've just had so many requests to hear it over and over again! But I'm sure we can add in some new tunes to our daily festivities," she lied. Snow White skipped off, believing every word of it. The good fairies had never lied to them before, so they surely wouldn't start now, or so she thought.

"Good fairies! While lovely, I can't concentrate on my book with this song playing over and over again," Belle exclaimed.

"I agree! It's nice to dance, but is it so necessary to only hear the same thing for such a long time now?" Wendy added.

The fairy godmothers looked at each other, worry prevalent on their faces. They did not know where the music was coming from, or what to do about it. One suggested they all just put their wands in the air and cast a silencing spell. However, no matter how hard they tried, or how many fairies assisted, they had no luck. Their wands were powerless against the song.

It's a small world after all.
It's a small world after all.
It's a small world after all.
It's a small world after all.

It's always at this point in the story where I would begin to question if the hero would prevail. It was my favorite part, and I had always dreamed of being right in the middle of such an adventure in a far-off kingdom. But now that it was actually here....

What would happen if the villains *did* win? With such a track record, I never thought it would be possible. There was no way. There was still time. Wasn't there?

"Has anyone discovered where this music is coming from?" Daisy asked. The others shook their heads.

"I've looked for a source everywhere, but it doesn't grow louder in any single part of the kingdom. It simply plays over and over again," Rose added.

"Well, who's the one that created it? Surely they know!" Lily said. No one spoke.

"Anyone?" Still nothing.

Finally, Rose spoke. "You don't think it could be the gift from those traveling royals, do you?"

Lily shook her head. "Trust me, I've already checked. But the sound isn't coming from the box at all. I had the same thought."

That was a bit of Her Majesty's handiwork. She had enchanted the necklace to produce the sound in a way that it would sound far away. It was a clever addition to the plan, one that I had not even thought of.

And a smile means friendship to everyone
Though the mountains divide, and the oceans are wide
It's a small world after all.

"Surely, they have to be tired of it by now," Vanessa said, as she was pacing the tavern. It was difficult just waiting, of course. Everyone wanted to know if the plan had been successful or not. Including me.

"The time will come, and that's when you enter," Her Majesty said, pointing to me.

I had almost forgotten that I still had a part to play in this story. Had I led myself down a rabbit hole that I wasn't sure I could follow? No, I had gone this far, there was no turning back now. I escaped from my thoughts just long enough to hear the end of Her Majesty's instructions.

"Lead them away from the kingdom, but it is important to do so quickly, so that they do not see us coming."

"If they do, this whole plan will have been for nothing," Hook warned.

I nodded. There really was no way out. The last thing you would ever want to do is cross the four most wicked villains in history—especially when you know what side of the barrier you're on.

We continued to watch, staring out the window, waiting for our next move. Patiently, as days passed, we waited.

"I can't stand it any more! That's all I hear all day long. *It's a small world, it's a small world!* I understand that it's small, do I need to hear it again?" Belle complained to a tired-looking Ariel.

"I just don't understand why it is still going on. Surely, there has to be a part of the kingdom without the music!"

"No, I've asked the good fairies, and they said they're searching everywhere, but no luck. Not in this kingdom," Snow White added.

"At this point, I don't really mind what kingdom I'm in. I just need complete silence," Belle sighed. She hadn't been able to enjoy a book in days, and it was driving her mad.

There's so much that we share
That it's time we're aware
It's a small world after all.

The song had been playing for three days now. Over and over again, it never paused, even for just a moment. Even with its joyful tune and beautiful rhymes, everyone could agree that after hearing it for the…. Oh, even I had lost count on how many times it had played; you just needed a moment to hear your own thoughts, to think, to process everything that was happening, to *realize* what was happening.

"It's time," I said, unsure if they really were my words coming out of my mouth. Why did I say that? Deep down, did I really want to go through with the whole plan? Or was I just trying to get it over with, knowing that prolonging it would only make it harder? Whatever the reason, the time had come, and the next phase of the plan was ready for action.

In almost an instant, we were back at the *Upstream Plunge,* and I was boarding along with the crew. They were going on and on, mostly discussing what they would do in their new home, how they would quickly change the cheerful decor to something more fitted to their tastes. I couldn't pay attention to any of it. All I could focus on was the slow approach of our boat across the water. With each skip over the wave, the villains were closer to what they had waited their whole lives for. To finally win.

And really, it was what I had always wanted, too. A story in which the hero doesn't always win, a story in which there is real conflict, and everything isn't perfect. I had dreamed of this for years, hoped for a world filled with a little mischief and chaos. But now that it was here…. Well, even a writer can second guess their own story.

"You know what to do?" Hook asked, snapping me back in to reality.

"Of course. As much as this song has been playing, I'll barely have to say hello before they board this ship," I said, feigning confidence.

As our boat moved closer, I could hear the song clearly now. It really was a happy little tune, so simple but with such a strong message. Even after the second time around, however, I could see how the villains' spell had been working. By the third time, my thoughts were starting to mesh together with the song, and I wasn't really sure what the difference between *it's a small world* and the chatter of the villains behind me was. Oh, they were tricky. They were wicked. They were *good* at being bad.

The boat stopped.

Now was the time. I would go in, do my part, and the ultimate arc of the story would commence. A story in which there is no perfect ending, in which the wicked would finally win. A story different than anything that had ever been done before. All I had to do was play the part, and cause the chaos.

Walking off the dock, I approached the border, this time alone. I could see the royals on the other side; their smiles had days ago faded from their faces, and not a single one of them was dancing. The fairy godmothers, who had clearly not slept the past three days, were still running around, looking for an answer, or a counter-spell, to fix all of this. I watched for just a moment. It really was chaos, right in the middle of this land of perfection. I felt a small smirk spread across my face, and I knew I was ready for the next part of the plan.

I waved frantically, at the edge of the barrier, with the most concerned look on my face that I could muster. A fairy godmother, who I had not met before, approached. She was accompanied by a knight. She waved her wand, creating a small door in the barrier, and they both walked toward me.

"Hello, my dear! I'm afraid we haven't met before," she said.

I nodded. "Yes, my name is Princess Emalina." The knight chuckled and pushed his glasses up on to his nose.

"I visited your kingdom a few days ago. Well, while visiting, I'm afraid I must have lost something. Something very dear to me, and I am hoping that it is here, and not lost at sea," I began. I think I even made a tear form in my eye, because the fairy godmother, who I later discovered was named Azalea, was now touching my shoulder.

"You see, it was a small compass. It belonged to my mother before, well, before I lost her. I know what you're thinking. Again? How cliché. But I had to play the part of a royal, didn't I? "It's the only thing I have of hers, and it really does mean so much to me."

"My dear, why don't we go in, have a look around, and ask the other fairies if they have seen your compass?" she said, putting her arm around me and walking me toward the barrier.

I hadn't thought this part through. The first time I had walked through, I hadn't truly done anything wicked. I hadn't cast Her Majesty's spell yet. I hadn't completely crossed over to the side of evil. What if I was pushed out now? Would she realize that I had been a part of this villainous plot all along, and then the whole thing would fall to shambles?

"Why don't I escort you, *Princess* Emilee?" The knight said, as I took his arm.

"Princess *Emalina*," I corrected him.

I could hear the song even louder now that I was on their side. Over and over again, the same words rang through my ears.

It's a small world after all.
It's a small world after all.
It's a small world after all.
It's a small, small world.
It's a world of laughter, a world of tears....

No wonder the royals looked so tired. After hearing that for days on end, how they were able to form a complete thought was beyond me. They were a lot stronger than I had imagined.

"What a lovely tune!" I said to Azalea, who took a deep breath before responding.

"It's a bit *much*, don't you think?" the knight said under his breath.

"Oh, do you like it? Our royals have just been so in love with it. We have been listening to it all day," she lied. Of course, she wouldn't want a visiting princess to think that their kingdom was falling apart. Could you imagine the rumors?

"It's truly wonderful. Our kingdom is so quiet, hardly any music fills the air like yours!" I said. I watched as the light filled Azalea's eyes.

"You don't say?" I could actually hear the wheels turning in her head. Our plan was already working.

"Indeed! We're a very peaceful kingdom, which usually means peaceful silence. It's quaint, quiet, and comfortable, I suppose." I laughed. Azalea nodded, her mind far too preoccupied with her own plan to even answer me.

There is just one moon,
And one golden sun.

We walked toward the center of the courtyard, and I took a moment to appreciate the kingdom for all its beauty. Everything seemed to glisten, every inch of it perfectly clean and sparkling. Bright blues contrasted against the grey—no, silver—bricks of the castle, overlooking a courtyard full of color and whimsy. It truly was a sight to see, a place so magnificent. And the royals were perfectly primped in colorful gowns that somehow seemed to coordinate with the décor. Perhaps it was a shame to trick them away....

And a smile means
Friendship to everyone.

"Princess Emalina! What a pleasure to see you again!" Rose said to me as we approached a group of fairy godmothers. The others, some that I had met before, and others that I had not, curtsied as I approached. I followed suit, smiling from ear to ear.

"Rosebud! Lily! Oh, even Daisy! How lovely to see you again!" Azalea explained why I was there, looking for the compass of my poor, lost mother. I nodded along, making sure I looked extremely worried. However, Azalea's topic of conversation quickly transitioned to the *quiet* kingdom that I had come from.

"Quiet, you say? As in, no music at all?" Daisy asked. She sounded so desperate.

"None at all! You should all come for a visit sometime." I said. Their smiles widened more than I had ever seen before.

"We wouldn't want to intrude. But, you know, it would be so nice to see one of the neighboring kingdoms." Lily said. The other fairies nodded in agreement.

"I think we should intrude immediately!" the knight said.

"Although, we may need to bring all of the inhabitants of our kingdom, you see," Rose added. She wasn't going to beat around the bush.

"Why is that?" I asked, playing the fool.

"Truth be told, Princess, that we believe our kingdom is under some sort of enchantment that even we can not undo. This beautiful song, kind as it is, is all that we can hear. Over and over again, for days!"

"We're quite a small kingdom, really. And it would only be until we can undo this magic," Daisy said.

"Oh, dear friends! This isn't even a question! Of course, gather everyone together. Do you have a magic mirror? I can call out to my dear Prince...Gastonaymous and have our people bring more boats to your shore!"

Though the mountains divide
And the oceans are wide
It's a small world after all.

In what seemed like the blink of an eye, there they were. Dozens of ships waiting at the port, captained by finely dressed pirates in disguise. They dropped their anchors as I stood next to a worried Belle, Ariel, Snow White, and Wendy Darling.

"What did you say your name was, dear?" Snow White asked.

"Princess Emalina."

"Funny, I've never heard of you before. Our kingdom has the stories of every royalty there ever has been in our library," Belle said.

"They must simply be the stories of the royals from *your* kingdom. Ours is such a forgotten little place, it often gets overlooked," I said. *Please, no more questions.*

"I think it's a wonderful adventure! I can't wait to see this new land!" Wendy said. It would certainly be an adventure. Far more of an adventure they could ever expect.

There we all stood, right before the barrier, waiting. You could barely see it, except for the glow of pixie dust that shined against the sunlight. I watched as the the glow of the pixie dust faded away as the last fairy godmother stepped outside the kingdom border.

The barrier was actually down. Even though I was watching it happen, I could not truly fathom what was going on.

"Quickly, now! We must reach our kingdom before nightfall; otherwise, rough seas will approach us, and we wouldn't want that," I instructed. Ariel nodded quickly. They all began to board the boats without even taking a moment to glance back at the kingdom they were leaving behind. Or without closing the barrier.

"Princess Emalina! Where is Prince...Prince...." one of the fairy godmothers started.

"Ah, Prince Gastonagaon! Well, I told him to stay in our kingdom to ensure everything was prepared for your arrival!"

"Prince Gastonagon?" Belle asked with a quizzical look on her face. I didn't even attempt an answer, I simply rushed over to one of the smaller boats, where a once scruffy-looking pirate was now assisting fair princesses on board. I watched as one by one, they moved away from their beloved kingdom, and toward a fate they couldn't even see coming.

It's a world of hopes,
And a world of fears.
There's so much that we share,
That it's time we're aware,
It's a small world after all.

"Aren't they all on board yet? What is *taking* them so long?" Gaston complained, watching from a far-off boat.

"Patience. Our time is nearly here," Her Majesty said.

They looked on, waiting with intense anticipation. With every click of the princesses' heels on the docks, it seemed like hours would pass by.

Finally, they saw the last boat pull away from the dock, and an empty kingdom now awaited them. They docked their own boat, and the four of them stood where the barrier once was. There was no shine, no glimmer of pixie dust. Nothing stood in their way. For once, nothing could stop them.

They took a step forward.

They made it.

They looked back, watching as the royalty sailed away, laughing and smiling. It was then that Vanessa caught a glimpse of Ariel, her red hair resting nicely on Prince Eric's shoulder. Her eyebrows scrunched together, her smile faded, and a scowl formed on her face. Quickly, that scowl turned to a smirk.

"I think these royals need a little *push* to reach their new home," she said. The villains smiled; they could never resist a little extra mischief.

Vanessa muttered an enchantment, calling upon the winds of the sea. The clouds darkened and swirled above the water. The waves began to rise and fall, quickly picking up speed, approaching the small fleet of ships.

I saw the water coming toward us. I shook my head. This was never a part of the plan that we had discussed. I knew something would happen. Someone's anger would get the best of them, and they would have to seek out their own revenge.

"Everyone! Hold on tightly! Get down!" I yelled to the group. The knight grabbed my hand as the first wave hit the boat.

I could hear the princesses screaming as they turned to see the massive waves approaching. The water violently hit the boats, rocking them from one side to the other. The princes bravely held on to the sides of the boat, but you could see the fear in their eyes.

Back and forth, the water kept hitting our small boats, ensuring panic with every movement. I watched as fairy godmothers tried to clear the skies with their magic, but they could not quite find a spell that would work. Every weather spell proved unsuccessful. Perhaps because it wasn't an act of *true* weather.

The water transitioned from pushing us from side to side, to pushing us forward. Faster and faster, the sails looked as if they were about the burst with the pressure from the winds. I knew where we were going. These villains didn't want a quiet disembark to the village. They wanted to make a show of it.

I saw the dock approaching; it surely wouldn't survive a dozen boats crashing in to it. I just hoped that we would. But the boats didn't slow down, no, they seemed to increase their speed as we inched closer and closer to the dock and the rocks that surrounded it.

"We're going to crash!" a princess screamed. In the chaos, I really couldn't tell you which one. Others cried and screamed. I think I even saw a prince shed a tear or two. Everyone held on to the boats tightly as we saw the crash coming....

Screams rang out as the boats hit the rocks in front of them. Princes were thrown from their seats. Princesses, with their soaked dresses, fell to the floor. However, not one fell overboard. Not one was hurt. No, I knew these villains wanted each and every passenger to see what was happening.

"Is everyone all right?" I called out. Groans answered as the collective response.

"Quickly, we must get off the boats! We don't know if they will sink. Hopefully this village will offer us shelter," I said, playing my part.

Along with my piratical, I mean, *princely*, crew, we helped everyone off of the boats. They all looked miserable, completely drenched and terrified. As I helped Snow White off the boat, she looked up at me and smiled.

"Princess Emalina, how do you remain so calm?" she asked. For a moment, I froze. I forgot that in all of this, I should have been as terrified as they were.

"Well, I just realized I needed to help. I suppose that made me forget my fears." I gave her a smile, and she hugged me.

"We all owe you for that! Thank goodness you are here for us!"

How quickly she trusted me. How quickly they all trusted me. I felt bad, really. A part of me thought to forget the whole thing, tell them that this was a trap that they had so easily fallen into. Wake up, princesses! See what's going on! But none of them did. They smiled, stepping out of the boats with the help of the crew, walking into a new land. Just like *that*. They simply believed that I was good and here to help them. Maybe I could; there was still time.

No, I had come this far. There was no turning back.

When no more fairies, princes, or princesses were left on the boats, my band of princely pirates followed along. Without any of the royalty noticing, they snuck off, running back toward the kingdom, following the water until they reached their new home. I was the last one to leave the docks. The royalty all just kept walking, waiting for a sparkling kingdom to appear in front of them.

When I heard the gasp of a princess in the crowd, I knew that Vanessa and Her Majesty had started the next part of the plan.

We all watched, as off in the distance, the kingdom seemed to *disappear*. Yes, actually disappear! They had done it.

Okay, they didn't really make an entire kingdom disappear.

They had cast a spell to make the kingdom *look* as if it had cvanished. The castle would be unrecognizable, the surrounding buildings like they weren't there at all. A perfect way to protect the villains' happily ever after.

The only thing we could see were large thorns that seemed to be growing from the ground, a touch that Her Majesty had borrowed from Maleficent, that circled where the kingdom once stood.

"What's happening?" a princess shrieked. The fairy godmothers all looked from one to the other. They were all in shock.

"Princess Emalina! You saved us! We were out of there just in time! Perhaps we would have all vanished as well! And hopefully this new kingdom will treat us with the same kindness that you have." Snow White said, as she hugged me for the second time. Even after all of this, they still trusted me. They still believed I had nothing to do with it. Perhaps I could continue that, start over as a princess with her knight, and go back to living the perfect life that I had grown up in....

"I'm not so sure about that," I heard Belle say. She was standing in front of the tavern. Finally, one of them had figured it out. She looked from the tavern over to the empty land where their Kingdom had once been.

"Impossible! But, where is everyone?!" a fairy godmother cried out. It did seem to be impossible. After so much work, so much planning, they had won. *We* had won.

I watched as they looked for the villains, and back at the empty space behind the thorns. They couldn't put it together, couldn't understand what was happening to them. *Why* it was happening to them.

"They've taken over our kingdom," Belle finally said. They all turned to each other, some of them arguing that it was impossible. But I watched as they started to put the pieces together and began to understand that this was actually happening.

"Who?!" Snow White gasped.

I had to make my choice. Still, none of them suspected me. I could stay with them, help them as I helped the wicked, maybe one day take back the kingdom. Or, I cross to the other side, ensuring that the land of chaos and mischief remained strong. Far from the world of perfection. Or, venture to another kingdom to start all over. My mind raced, faster than any of the concerned royals and fairy godmothers around me.

"Everyone! I'm not sure what's going on, but I intend to go get help. There is one ship that seems to be all right, and it hasn't suffered much damage. I will sail to a neighboring kingdom, a *good* Kingdom, to see if they might help us."

"It's a very dangerous journey back. I will go with you," the knight said.

"You're such a hero!" Rose exclaimed. Everyone cheered and applauded. They still trusted me. I could use that later.

As promised, the villains had left a small opening in the thorns, off to the far side of the kingdom. Once the knight and I passed through, Her Majesty would seal it, entangling the thorns together to create a tight lock. They stood there, waiting for me on the other side. As we approached, I saw the smiles on their faces, the excitement in their eyes. We walked through, and the thorns quickly grew together behind me.

Once it was closed, the celebrating began. LeFou's Brew, which, of course, was brought over from their little village, was passed around, and cheers could be heard from every corner.

"We finally won! A kingdom of our very own!" Vanessa cheered.

"A castle fit for true royalty!" Her Majesty agreed.

"A kingdom almost as beautiful as me!" Gaston added.

"It truly is the happiest of things, as difficult as it is to say," Hook added, making everyone laugh.

"We thank you, *Princess Emalina*, for without you, this would not have been possible," Her Majesty said. I curtsied to her gracefully, slightly knocking the tiara off of my head.

"Please—it's just Emilee," I said.

It didn't take long for the kingdom to lose its shine and sparkle. Even though the outside world could not see it, we still could. Pirates raised their flags atop their buildings, ruffians and thugs "redecorated" the proper buildings into places more suitable for their tastes. And, perhaps I was seeing things, but it almost seemed like a thick haze was falling over the kingdom. And then, of course, there was the castle.

"Well, as the only true queen, it's only fitting that I live in the castle," Her Majesty had argued.

"Do you see anywhere else in this kingdom fit for me? No, I must live in the grandest of places!" Gaston cried out. They all had their arguments as to who should live there, and why.

It was easy to see why they all wanted it. It was the only part of the kingdom that hadn't started to look like their old, rundown village. Her Majesty had declared that the castle would be untouched, as it was a shining reminder that they had taken this land from the royals, and it could never change. Even though none of them ever wanted to admit it, they all wanted to be royalty.

However, there was a bigger issue than just the living arrangements. There was still a song playing over and over and over again. Surely, it would wear off quickly enough, leaving us with the land that we had all dreamed of.

It's a small world after all.

And what of the royals, you might ask? Well, the princesses worked tirelessly to clean up the village, as they knew I was not returning. There were rumors that perhaps I really was wicked, but many of the princesses refused to believe it. Some of them said I must have been lost at sea, or perhaps I was taken captive in a nearby land. No one was quite sure what had happened to poor Princess Emalina or the brave knight, but they knew that they were going to be stuck in their village for quite some time.

They decided to make the best of it, making this uninhabited land their new home. The dusty old tavern now seemed to have a simple charm to it, and almost looked...*clean.* The kingdom, which they were now calling New Fantasyland, was growing every minute, Fairy godmothers built magnificent palaces around the small tavern. It shown beautifully, especially compared to what it had been before. The princesses had returned to a joyful life of dancing with their handsome princes, no matter where their kingdom might be. Joyful music filled the air, with sweet songs of finding their true love echoing throughout the land.

Two weeks later, and we could not say the same thing. It's all we could hear. Day in and day out. Vanessa worked tirelessly on getting rid of the necklace, but somehow it still ended up back, the song playing over and over again.

It's a world of laughter,
A world of tears.
It's a world of hopes,
And a world of fears.
There's so much that we share,
That it's time we're aware,
It's a small world after all.

Her Majesty tried retracting the spell. She never seemed to look up from her spellbook, trying every enchantment that she could find. Gaston tried breaking Vanessa's necklace, but that only seemed to aggravate it, and we swear that it almost made the song grow louder. This was what we had worked so hard for. This was the happily ever after that we were now stuck with.

But like all good stories, happily ever after is only the beginning.

The Adventures of Mr. Tom Morrow

a Tomorrowland short story by Patrick Kling

"Paging Mr. Morrow, Mr. Tom Morrow: Please contact Mr. Johnson in the control tower to confirm your flight to the moon."

That was the third time this week that I had been paged for a "flight to the moon." I was on my morning run at the time. I liked to run around our city's space port. All of the hustle and the bustle of the port gave me energy and life. It really does take a lot of work to look this good. Also, I had constant inspiration from the people, the objects, and the chaos. I had other reasons to run in the space port, or what we affectionately called Space Mountain. People were always in a hurry, they were late for flights, they had places to be. Here, I could run and not be stopped for photos from my adoring fans.

Wait a second.... Out of the corner of my eye I saw something interesting, the Space Rockets. They were backing up in the return tunnel...a cascading of sorts. I initiated my Shoeblaster 3,000 (patent pending) to fly me over as quickly as possible to the main console of the return dock. The panicky crowd cheered my arrival. I hoped it wasn't a Morrow, Inc. computer issue.

"Mr. Morrow, thank goodness you are here, we are having an issue with the computers!" the console crew member exclaimed.

"What are we going to do!? This is a disaster," another crew member chimed in.

"No need to fret, kind citizens. I'm here to save the day!?" I proclaimed confidently while striking a victory pose. After a few necessary rounds of applause from the fans, I got to work examining the computer. Our computers were pretty reliable, but it is hard to account for user error.

"Hurry!" a crew member shouted.

"We're all gonna die!?!?!" a vexatious onlooker screamed.

I took out my phone.

"Did you know that there is enough processing power to launch a space shuttle in your phone? I hope. Cross your fingers."

I plugged my phone into the console and quickly overtook the command dispatching rockets through.

"Looks like it's working," I said with a wink.

The rockets began advancing and the crowd roared with applause. No matter how many times the fair citizens chant my name, I simply still can't get enough.

"Now about the computer issue." I rubbed my finger across the console; it was sticky. I took a whiff and tasted my finger.

"Hmm...is that Coca Cola I taste?"

"Ye—yes, sir," the crew members replied.

"Looks like the monitor is fried, but the system is still working. Just call it in. Oh, and feel free to keep the phone as a memento for meeting me." I had several phones on hand for situations like this.

"Th-thank you, sir. It is truly an honor."

"It is, isn't it?"

The thankful citizens chanted my name throughout the spaceport. I had to address my adoring fans; it is a part of the job.

"Everything is going to be all right! While it is true I saved the day in this moment, I assure you that the Morrow, Inc. Control System has everything under control!" The chanting began to subside, so I cupped my ear as a playful call for the crowd to cheer again.

"I can't hear you!" I really could not get enough of this!

Despite my theatrics, this was an easy task to complete. Usually when I save the day it is more...*interesting*. I assure you.

Where was I? Oh, right. I knew basically everyone in town. They were my investors, my supporters, my consumers. My father started a technology company called Morrow, Inc. and it exploded. Well...not exploded literally, it expanded rapidly. You can look around your house right now and I guarantee that our company has had a hand in creating it. Even this book you're reading was printed on a Morrow machine and distributed to you via a Morrow drone. The City of Tomorrow was my father's grand experiment, where everything would be perfect. All of his inventions could be put to good use. It was a new start, completely new infrastructure without the burdens of the relics of the past. The inception of the City of Tomorrow is a rather fascinating story, but a story for another time.

The City of Tomorrow...it worked out kind of okay. Regardless, when you're the son of the founder of the city you live in, and you are the city's treasure, saving them day in and day out, and are tall, with stunning blue eyes and physical features (if I do say so myself), people are going to know you. My now elderly father, Mr. Tom Morrow, liked naming things after him so much he named me after him as well.

Now you might be thinking that the whole rocket cascade was what I was needed for that day, but you're wrong. It was something else. My talents were expansive and this was merely an example of what I happen to do on my morning run. Nevertheless, I headed toward the control tower. The control tower they were talking about was at city hall, right in the heart of the City of Tomorrow. I had my own private entrance, with my own private elevator that would take me straight to the governor's office. They knew how to treat a hero like myself.

As the proprietor of the biggest technology firm, and son of the founder and builder of the city, it wasn't too unusual for me to be in the control tower frequently. As you must've gathered by this point, I am simply exceptional and in high demand. Now, I won't pretend to tell you that I knew today was going to be different. It makes for a better story, but this was simply not the case. I treated it like every other day. Well, if there was any difference it was that I decided to run instead of taking my hovermobile.

I entered to find both Governor Johnson and Police Commissioner Mitchel at the conference table of the sleek office, looking concerned.

"Good morning, Mr. Morrow. We have a bit of a doozy here this morning," the governor said.

"I don't think it is a doozy, we have it under control...." Commissioner Mitchel began.

"You do *not*," the governor interrupted.

Oh boy, here was my first hint that this day was going to be different. The two of them had a lot of history. Mitchel had once fancied herself to be governor, but she wasn't good at the politics game. Going the police route was also a challenge. When you run a department there is bound to be scandal, poor decisions that result in life or death. The route Mrs. Johnson had taken was a lot less...controversial. All she had to do was show up for a legislation signing, kiss a few babies, and cut the ribbon at the opening of Auntie Gravity's ice cream parlor.

"What'll it be today? Did a carnivorous Alien escape at X-S Tech? They should really shut that place down," I quipped.

"No aliens, we think the Fox has resurfaced. We have intelligence that leads us to the Fox using the Merchant of Venus as a front for heinous activity. We believe their next hit will be Tomorrowland Intergalactic Bank. We think they hit the Hover Hotel last week," the governor said.

"We have things under control," Commissioner Mitchel added.

"Oh, I am sure you do, Commissioner, but sometimes it's best to have help from a guy like me. Can you give me a few minutes to look over all of the data you have on the Fox?" I asked.

"Of course. Mitchel will give you the overview," the Governor replied.

I didn't need to see any of the details. I *knew* what the Fox was up to. Robbing from the rich to give to the poor, a modern-day Robin Hood. I feigned interest in the presentation. While the officials had no idea who the Fox was, I did.

This seems like a good place to tell you a little bit more about myself. I was the runner of the business by day, and a vigilante crime fighter at night. Even such a technologically advanced city had crime, and with those buffoons at X-S still in operation, there was never a shortage of people needing my services. "Vigilante" might be a bit of a strong word. I had the full support of the governor; however, the police commissioner wasn't too keen on having an independent, intelligent, handsome hero like myself constantly swooping in to rescue her department. My father figured crime would be a thing of the past. But by golly, there simply are a few bad apples out there. The presentation ended.

"Mr. Morrow, if you need any resources from our police team, let us know."

"I will keep it in mind," I politely stated. Those on the police force were good at many things, but finding the Fox was not one of them. They left the room and I was free to peruse at my own speed, which was quick. This one was a doozy, but more on that later.

I had to make up time, so I hopped on the PeopleMover to catch a ride home. I needed to talk to my wife, Mindy, Mrs. Morrow. I wanted to chat with her before work that morning. Can you believe this all happened before 8:00 am?

We had a pretty illustrious condo at the top of Morrow Tower, the most luxurious residence in town. Someone had to live the good life, right? I had already broken the seal on my Shoe Blaster 3,000s, so I decided to fly to the top of the building instead of taking the elevator. My wife was in the kitchen eating some hydroponically grown bacon, as I burst through the balcony window triumphantly.

"Hey, honey, using the boots today, eh?"

She gave me a morning kiss. She was amazing, daring, and intelligent. My perfect match. Mrs. Morrow was a brilliant inventor, and to be honest, at least two-thirds the brains of the operation. So much of an innovator and an inventor that my father had installed her as the chief innovention officer several years ago. The title was confusing to many. Nonetheless, every other week she would have another gizmo for me to play with.

"How was your run?"

"Stopped a cascade at Space Mountain, got called to the control tower to hear about another mission, and grabbed some Starbucks. So you know, the usual stuff," I said with a smile.

"What's the mission?"

"You're not going to believe it. The Fox has resurfaced."

"Did you say *the Fox*!?"

"Yup."

"Wow. Back after all these years."

"They think she is targeting the Tomorrowland Intergalactic Bank for something. I am not really sure what to do about it yet. What do you think?" I asked her.

"First, you need to get to the bottom of it, see what she's really up to. Is she in town?"

"Yes, apparently underneath the Merchant of Venus."

"Go talk to her tonight and see what you can find out. Oh, and please do tell her I said hello."

My wife was amazing, always knew what to do. Okay, so maybe she was three-fourths of the brains of the operation.

It had been awhile since the Fox and I had talked. She had ventured off in the galaxy, and I was a bit disappointed that she hadn't reached out to me upon her return.

In the evening, after countless conference calls and executive meetings, I hopped in my hovermobile and flew to the Merchant of Venus store. It was full of intergalactic goodies. I took out my trusty 9D-Optical Scanning Remote, and scanned the interior for a secret entrance to the lair. I went through the back storage room quickly, not interacting with the shopkeeper. *Aha!* The secret panel to enter was in the fridge. I hated the cold. With a pop of the hatch, I lowered myself in.

I let go of the ladder and fell graciously to the floor. It may not have been too graceful, but I walked away with only minor damage. The lair was abandoned, completely powered down. I used my remote again to find the power-source to light it up. I found the master control and entered a few passwords. *Tom Morrow.* it worked. Yup, she could be that obvious sometimes.

A klaxon alarm wailed. I was the rube. The Fox would be there shortly. I donned my noise-cancelling headphones, put on some Beethoven, and awaited her arrival.

"This building will self destruct in 90 seconds...."

Oops.

Metal bars came crashing down, blocking the exit hatch. The music was quite pleasant. Ah, the retinal scanner. With a few keystrokes, the master override had been initiated. The scanner bleeped and blooped over my eyes.

"Hello, Tom."

"Complete destruction in 10... 9... 8... 7..."

This one was a bit of a pickle. I took a seat on the desk in the corner.

"4... 3... 2... 1... 1... 1..."

The Fox had a sense of humor. All the lights turned off, and my devices were deactivated. *Did I just blow up?* The lights and machines snapped back on.

There she was at the master control panel, typing away. She was siting in the most elegant of super-villain chairs I had ever seen in my life.

The Fox spun around ever so slowly.

"I've been expecting you."

"You know that's pretty cliché."

"Are we alone?" she asked.

"Yup, bring it in here for the real deal." I gave her a big hug. It had been awhile.

"It's been too long."

"So what's the Fox been up to all these years? Robbing from the so-called evil corporations and giving those riches to the less fortunate?"

"Yeah, thats about right."

One might wonder what I was doing cuddling up with the most infamous "villain" in all of Tomorrowland. The Fox was my younger sister. *Dun, dun, DUN.* She had a different world view. I had been groomed to take over the company, while she was interested in righting the wrongs of society by any means necessary. Our apples didn't fall too far apart from one another. Our motives were the same, but we believed in different methods to accomplish them. My sister wasn't a bad apple. I thought she was just misguided with the way she operated.

"So what's my big brother been up to all these years? Developing dangerous technology, selling them to the highest war criminals, all off the backs of underpaid workers?"

"If you'd like to voice your concerns for our workers' pay, I recommend you show up at a board meeting, a shareholder meeting, or even Thanksgiving dinner to discuss your issues with the family business. You own a third of the business, don't forget that."

Her set up was a bit paradoxical. My sister would use her company dividends to operate her so-called "evil" operation.

We weren't too different, her and I. I would use my dividends and annual salary to run my crime-fighting operation. Despite not liking the politics, or the idea of a corporation existing at all, she gained quite a bit from it. She had spread relative *good* throughout the galaxy, though.

"Alright, so what are we doing here?" she asked.

"It's not to invite you to the annual family picnic. However, we would love it if you could come."

She scowled. While we kept a good humor with one another sometimes, a lot of times I would push her buttons.

"The governor and police commiss...."

"Those corrupt, corporate...." she countered.

"Yes."

"Scum."

"Yes, them. They think you are targeting the Tomorrowland Intergalactic Bank for a heist. They know you are under here, and they think you broke into the Hover Hotel last week. They don't know why you did it, but I have a hunch you were getting retinal...."

"They still don't know who I am?"

"No."

"Good, we can simply walk out the front door, then," she said as she pressed a button on her watch.

"This building will self destruct in 10... 9... 8..."

"Can you just erase your damn computers? Why are we blowing up buildings now?"

"Fine, but you owe me," she begrudgingly stated. With a beep and a blap, the sequence was terminated.

"How about dinner and a place to stay while you're in town?"

"Let's start with dinner," she said.

"I'll let Mrs. Morrow know you'll be joining us."

She refused to take the PeopleMover, as she believed it was a job-killer, since it was basically an autonomous system. So much of the city was automated, but she preferred to ride around on her bicycle. I ran beside her.

"Did you know that you're expelling more energy and calories riding that bike right now than it would to ride on the PeopleMover?" I jested. It was true, you can look it up on morrowpedia.com. (I'll wait.)

She scowled at me again. Sometimes being a do-gooder was counter-intuitive.

We made it to our home, and she burst through the door. She looked around at our various art pieces and devices. She shook her head.

"Wow, look at all this...*waste*. How could you live in a warehouse like this? I think I'm going to vomit."

Mrs. Morrow entered from the office. "Wow, it has been so long. Too long." They embraced for a sincere hug.

"Are you still keeping him in line?" my sister asked.

"Oh, of course." Their jokes were usually at my expense.

"I am going to start dinner, should be ready in 20 minutes. You two should catch up," I stated.

I enjoyed cooking. I loved creating, and I was pretty good at it, if I may say so. We had some very interesting advancements in food science at our company, and I figured tonight would be the perfect night to showcase them. I prepared an amazing feast, chicken cordon bleu with a delectable cranberry and nut salad to start. I peeked in from the kitchen to the great room.

"You all ready? Dinner is served."

We gathered in the dinning room.

"I present to you a delicious cranberry and nut salad with a red wine vinaigrette dressing." My sister did a thorough investigation of the salad, ensuring it was organic and animal-free. She'd never heard of the expression, "Don't look a gift horse in the mouth." Most people haven't, to be honest.

"This tastes great," she finally admitted.

"Why, thank you. I learned to serve only the healthiest ingredients from you. Did you know we have been rapidly expa...."

"Save it for the press conference," she interrupted.

If my eyes could roll any further, I'd be looking at my gigantic brain.

"How is Dad?" my sister asked.

"He's great. He's still active. You know him, off at a charity event, or off on the board of directors for some charity throughout the galaxy, holding court with the elite around the universe. He'd love to hear from you."

"That's good to hear," she replied.

A silence swept over the table. My sister had been at odds with our dad for a very long time. He's a different man now, though. He was a bit ruthless growing up, a workaholic renegade willing to push his workers to extreme lengths, never willing to congratulate a person directly. He seemed a bit mysterious to all who knew him. We were the closest to him growing up, even though he was distant. My sister got the renegade aspects of him, and I got the workaholic part. I think we know how to handle our feelings, for the most part. I left the table to grab the main course from the oven.

"Chicken cordon bleu with a hint of rosemary, and scalloped Tritarien potatoes drizzled with Morrow cheese." I was proud.

"It looks and smells delicious," my wife said with delight.

"I can't eat this. I am a vegan, have been for years," my sister stated.

"Aha! Every piece of this dinner has absolutely *zero* animal product in it! The future is now!" I stated with glee.

"So all this was cooked up in some genetically modified hell lab. No, thank you."

"This is completely ethical. I thought you would be delighted. Our company is at the forefront of ending the slaughter of billions of creatures throughout the galaxy. You inspired me to invest in this division. Would you at least try it?"

"Fine." She took a bite of the chicken.

"Mmm, that's so good. Wow, I can't believe you did this. This is amazing."

"I was just kidding. It's actually a real chicken," I said with a grin.

"*What?!* You jerk!"

"No, no, no it's *really* genetically engineered."

"You promise? I can't eat this anymore."

"It really is genetically engineered. I led this division in the initial stages," my wife chimed in.

"Or *is* it?" I jested.

"Tom! Knock it off!" my wife scolded.

"Ok, it definitely is engineered. ... Or *is* it?"

My sister stormed out of the room, with my wife following behind. Maybe I took it too far this time. Oh, well, more cordon bleu for me. My wife calmed her down, and she came back.

"Despite your jokes, I really do appreciate what you have done here," my sister said. I gave her a hug.

She devoured the meal. Wouldn't you after not eating meat for several years? But it was time to move on to business. We went to the balcony and soaked in the beautiful view of the city.

"So, Tom tells me you might be working on a new project," my wife said.

"Yeah, you could call it that," my sister said with a chuckle. The hologram phone rang.

"Hold that thought. It's the governor and the commissioner calling," I plopped my phone on the table and a hologram formed. It was pretty cool technology we had invented a few years ago. My idea, of course.

"Ahoy there," I said.

"Sorry to bug you so late. Our SWAT team...is that your sister Angelica I see sitting there?" the commissioner asked.

"As a matter of fact, it is. She just got in tonight and will be staying with us for a few weeks before returning to school. We're really proud of her," I proclaimed. That statement had a lot of lies, even for me.

"Oh, excellent. Is she still attending that comic-book design school out in the Shantorou region?

"Oh, yes, I've had a great semester, and am actually nearing completion of my first comic book," Angelica stated.

"Well, isn't that nice. We don't want to interrupt you during your dinner. Why don't we call you back?" the governor said.

"Plus, we'd prefer to talk to you in *private*," the commissioner added.

"Oh of *course*. I'll call you back in a moment in a private setting."

I hung up and moved into my office. I brought my sister and wife with me, but out of view of the hologram phone.

"Okay, the line is secure. What's the latest?"

"Our SWAT team raided the Merchant of Venus a few minutes ago and we found an underground lair. All computers had been wiped and we now have absolutely no leads. What do you make of it?" the commissioner asked.

"Maybe the Fox decided to stop their current plan." My sister gave me a knowing shake of her head. It was worth a shot.

"I stopped over there earlier this evening, but I wasn't able to power up any of the computers. I didn't find any other information worth pursuing,"

"Nothing at all?" the governor asked.

"And you didn't think to tell us...." the commissioner added.

I put the phone on mute.

"Angelica, you need to give me something here."

"Tell them you found a calendar that said I was going to strike Saturday day, Saturday night, or something like that."

"I didn't want to report until I had more facts. I did find something; a note on the wall, it had Saturday's date on it, might be the night of the heist."

"Why, that's this weekend!" the governor blurted.

"Precisely. I'd say you get your team ready. We'll need full SWAT protocol to capture the Fox once and for all!"

"Thank you very much, Mr. Morrow, we'll get right on it," the commissioner replied.

"Have a good night. I'd like to get back to my family," I said and hung up the phone.

This would keep them off the scent for a little bit. There was no way my sister was *actually* going to rob a bank on the day she says she would. I looked up from the table, to my wife.

"Where did she go?" My sister had vanished without a trace.

"This is so typical of her. She just wanders off right when we need her. I can't believe thi...."

"I'm in the restroom, you blockhead," she screamed.

My wife and I went out to the balcony.

"What do you make of this?" I queried.

"Angelica's not going to hang out for very long. We should let her spread her wings, and we'll let her come back to us. I don't think she would have gotten discovered had she not needed something from us," my wife astutely stated. She was always four steps ahead.

"Okay, sounds like a plan."

Moments later my sister burst from the bathroom.

"Did you wash your hands?" I teased.

"Of course, don't be gross."

I loved this.

"Oh, really? What color is the soap?"

Her face drew a blank; she had no idea.

"I really appreciate your hospitality, Mindy, but I must be going...."

"Oh, that's no problem," my wife replied.

"It was great seeing you; don't be a stranger. The Morrow company picnic is actually next month, or two months away, you should attend. Dad would love it," I added.

"Oh, okay, I will leave you to it, then." Angelica made her way slowly toward the door.

"Bye," my wife and I said in unison.

"It's not *too* late. I guess I could stay for another drink."

"Oh, no, no, no, it's getting late. If you need to be somewhere *else* tonight, then you really should be going. No reason to be out late if you can't spend the night," my wife stated.

I could tell Angelica felt dejected. Good. Who does she think she is, anyway, coming into my city and getting everyone all riled up?

"Okay. I guess I will leave then. Goodbye."

My wife guided her out the door. Angelica had *finally* left. I needed to unwind and digest everything that had happened.

"Honey, I need to...."

"I know. You need to go see Sonny," she interrupted.

"You're the best."

"Can you possibly have a lower profile and take the elevator this time?"

Later that evening, I arrived at Cosmic Ray's. I had phoned ahead and they had my table right up at the front. There I could hear Sonny Eclipse's standards. He was a one-man show you wouldn't want to miss.

Yew Nork...Yew Nork.. Yew Nork...

He was an old-school crooner. Out of this world, really. He had the soul of a poet and the humor of a slice of pepper jack cheese, aged 45 years. When I needed to unwind from a stressful or puzzling day, this is where I would go. I kept a classy profile. They had my usual drink at the table within moments of me sitting down.

At that moment, all I could think about was what Angelica was up to. Why did she take up residence underneath the

Merchant of Venus? Why did she want to get caught? Why didn't she ever wash her hands after using the bathroom? All important questions that I needed answers to.

Sonny finished his last tune for the hour, then swung by my table for our usual talk.

"You know, Sonny, it looks like you've been up on that stage for several decades. How do you do it?" It was my usual joke.

"What's on your mind today? Forget it. I read about it in the news. You rocketed to the top of the headlines today with your big save at Space Mountain."

"A little more than that happened today."

"Let me guess, an alien escaped at X-S Tech? They should really shut that place down...." he began.

"No, I am sure that did happen, though."

"Did you invent something at the *lab*? Something that is causing you to *bark*?" he asked.

"A dog pun, cute...but no...this is far more expansive. The Fox has returned." He knew Angelica's true identity. They were close. It's a long story.

"My ex-fiancée's returned, eh?"

I guess it was a short story.

"How is my sweet flower doing? Does she want me back? She and I were like glue and flowers. We stuck together and looked beautiful. She *pedaled* away. I never thought I'd love again after Luna, but then Angelica came into my life...."

"With all due respect Sonny, I'm not here to dive into your love life...or lack thereof."

"You know how to cut deep, Tom, real deep."

"Angelica could get herself into a lot of trouble here. The police are on to the Fox...."

"You don't think the police are really within reach, do you?" he asked.

"I am worried. They are onto her, and she's not doing a good job covering her tracks. This seems bigger than usual. I am not sure what she is up to yet."

"Maybe she is doing what she feels is right, and not politically convenient?" he slyly questioned. It was a dig against me.

"That's what she always does, but this time it could be too hard for me to protect her."

"What do you need from me?"

"Keep a look out. If she tries to talk to you, please let me know. She doesn't have many friends out here she can trust, but I know she trusts you," I stated.

"That I can do. But now I need to get ready for my next set. Any requests?"

"Just play the same stuff you always do. Why try and change a masterpiece?"

I finished my drink, and took in a few more of Sonny's hits before heading home on the PeopleMover and calling it a night.

It was a beautiful morning. The sun was rising over the horizon. I laced up my shoes and began my morning run. As usual, I headed toward Space Mountain. It was early, not too much action yet. I was about halfway to Space Mountain when I felt someone behind me. You know when you can just *feel* someone? That's what it was. I don't like that feeling. Not. One. Bit.

I spun around. There he was. How could he keep up? Could have been a fluke. I picked up my pace; no one could outrun me. I changed direction, toward the central PeopleMover station. He turned, too. I looked behind me to assess the threat. No weapon, no room for anything, just a person in the distance. I couldn't make our his face. It wasn't the first time I have been chased by a goofball idiotically trying to outrun me. I picked up the pace a bit more. He was actually gaining on me. Time to make some evasive maneuvers. I ran up the PeopleMover ramp onto the track. I would need to move quickly to avoid triggering an emergency stop of the system. I leapt over the first trigger point. I had the grid memorized. My potential assailant jumped off the ramp onto the track right along with me.

Enough of this. It's time for *parkour*!

I fled toward the oncoming PeopleMovers and leapt over them, while doing back flips, front flips, and side spins. There was no chance I would be outmatched by anyone, ever. Period. I swung onto the top of the PeopleMover roof and sprinted to the Astro Orbiter. The rockets were spinning fast. With a click of my Morrow, Inc. watch, I overrode the computer and made them spin faster. I leapt on top of a rocket.

The assailant had kept up.

"What do you want from me?!" I bellowed down.

He ignored me and kept up the pace, leaping from rocket to rocket. Faster and faster the rockets went, and faster and faster we leapt. It had only been a minute or so when it happened. *Phhhhsssssssshhhh*.... The rockets all lowered. I *had* to meet this guy.

I calmly got off the rocket I had been standing on. I'll admit it, I was out of breath. He confidently approached me.

"Well?" I shouted.

She took off her mask. It was Angelica.

"I need your help."

"You know, you *do* have my phone number. Don't you think that's a nicer way to approach me when you need my help?"

"What would be the fun in that?" She had a point.

"What is it you need me for?"

"I can't talk about it here. We need to meet in a neutral place. A place where nobody would think to look or wire tap. Go clean yourself up and await further instructions. And don't tell *anyone*."

I wasn't used to being told what to do. I was always the one calling the shots. I nodded and headed home. What would she want from me? What's with all the theatrics? When did she learn how to do parkour? All of these questions were flurrying through my head.

I arrived at home. Angelica wanted me to keep this hush-hush. I would have to avoid Mindy. I hopped in the shower, brushed my teeth, and dressed. I stared at my phone while I tied my tie. The phone buzzed right on cue.

her: meet me at the place where it all started.

me: I don't know where that is.

her: Seriously?

me: Yes.

her: Fine. Meet me where the space meets the sky.

me: I literally have no idea what you are talking about.

her: Meet me on top of Space Mountain!!!!!!!

me: k.

I took off my numerous communication devices and strapped on my Shoe Blasters 3000. As I was about to fly off the balcony, my wife peered around the corner and shook her head.

"If you had wings."

Within a few moments I was atop Space Mountain. There was no sign of Angelica. With no communication devices to look at, I was forced to stand there with nothing to do. Idling like a complete sap. My brain contemplated the meaning of life. Why we were all here? All those types of things rapidly flowing through my head like Niagara Falls. It had only been 48 seconds and I was about to crack.

"I've been expecting you," Angelica said as she appeared around a rooftop spire.

"Of course you have. You called me?! Now what is this all about?"

I had played her little games; now it was time for her to give me answers. She took out a scanner and gave my body a zap.

"I don't have any devices on me." I was getting irritated.

She began her eloquent speech: "You and I aren't so different. We both want good in the world and beyond our galaxy. I have been far and wide and...and I have discovered something very disturbing. The Tomorrowland Intergalactic Bank appears to be a massive money-laundering syndicate funneling and transferring money between horrible people throughout the galaxy...."

"So we go to the commissioner and the governor to handle...."

"I have reason to believe the governor and commissioner know about it."

"Well, then, we take them down. We impeach and expel them."

"No! We can't let them know that we know. There are hundreds of criminals that we could potentially track throughout the galaxy with this bank in place as it is now!" she blurted.

"That's unethical. I can't work day in and day out with criminals who...."

"Think big picture, Tom. We could wipe out hundreds of criminals across the galaxy. You've spent your entire life protecting corporate interests, and here you see the product of that. A corporation benefiting off of horrible people. The bank is happy to look a blind eye as they make millions from those billions they are funneling. And the governor, he takes his cut, too. I need your help, you need to impla...."

"Implant a virus in the bank system so that we can track where the dirty money is coming and going."

"Precisely!" Sonny Eclipse peered from behind my shoulder.

"Sonny, she's got you roped into this, too?" I asked, knowing the answer.

"She's right, honey." Honey? I turned around. It was my wife, Mindy.

"Is this an intervention?"

"All of us have the power to do something right here, and we can't do it without you," Angelica said.

"I need time to think about this, there might be another way...."

"The police believe we are going to attack on Saturday, but we must strike tomorrow night. I have intel that Sherock Dwendleson of the Choeorog Galaxy is planning a humongous transaction, and we need to track it. He's smuggling creatures to be used as slaves throughout the galaxy, and we must put an end to it. If we tip our hand to anyone else, it might be too late," Angelica said.

Here I was being ganged up on by my family and friends. They were on to something here. How far up did the corruption go? Were the commissioner and the governor really in on this? What would be their benefit? How could all of this go untraced in the software? We had the best people working in our cyber security sector. Were they in on it, too? These questions raced through my head. I thought about every interaction I had with our cyber division. I thought about every divisional vice president, every manager, every supervisor, every employee, even our robotic waste bins that come directly to us. Were they corrupted?

"Tom!" my wife shouted. I had been staring off into the distance, sometimes I just need to compose my thoughts. Sometimes I need to....

"*TOM!*" she screamed.

"There has to be something bigger going on here. Do you really think this could work?" I asked the group. "We're supposed to implant a virus, spy on the bank unnoticed, and go against all our company values, morals, protocols, and mission, jeopardizing ther entire company?"

"Yes!" Angelica, Mindy, and Sonny replied in unison.

"Well, we better get started, then," I said confidently. More like I acted confident; I wasn't sure of anything yet. We needed to go to where it was safe. Not my normal safe room; it needed to be safe from the government, safe from the people of Morrow, Inc, safe from prying eyes where nobody would ever go: the Tomorrowland Community Theater.

"Don't you think that's a little excessive?" Angelica asked.

Sonny was equally unamused. "Do we really need to go there?"

"It's the only way. I insist."

We went our separate ways. It would be no easy task to go undetected, but once at the theater we would be clear. My wife and I left together and returned home. I didn't feel like talking. It's rare that my wife and I aren't in alignment. I would have appreciated a tip-off. When did she know about this crackpot plan? When did Sonny know? I was in my head, and when I am in my head I need to process my feelings. With them straying away from me and withholding information I felt alone. I was frustrated, confused, powerless. Normally I was calling the shots, and in this case I was not. I felt vulnerable, I felt like I could lose everything at a moment's notice if the plan went astray. Every possible scenario of how this could play out rolled through my mind, and the outlooks were not good. It was all too risky, far more risky than I am comfortable with in my line of work. *Powerless.* My wife sat in the living room doing a bit of research on the intergalactic bank. I stared off to the balcony.

When it was time, I sent an alert out to the new team. We reconvened at the community theater. My sister set up the holograph equipment and Sonny was unloading blueprints, files, and tablets. We gathered around the table, a make-shift command room. Angelica took the lead pulling up information on our Morrow, Inc. hologram screens.

"Is this a closed-circuit system?" I asked. Sonny and Mindy turned toward Angelica.

"We have no time for sloppy work. If any computers are connected to any internet connection this plan could be completely compromised."

"Of course it is." She hesitated. I could see it in her eyes.

"The stakes couldn't be higher. You're risking everything for everyone in this room! This isn't something you can play fast and loose with. We need to be careful."

I know it sounds a bit harsh, but her trademark had been to get sloppy, get almost discovered, and truth be told, I have helped her out over the years too many times. This was her show, though. I wasn't running it, but I knew I needed to protect my friends and family, including her.

"I've come a long way, Tom," Angelica told me.

"Then surely you disengaged the security alarm for the theater?"

"Can we get on with this?" Sonny chimed in. I am used to having him on my side, my back, and everything else. With this project, I didn't know where his allegiance lied. Maybe there weren't any sides anymore. At this point, I didn't know.

Sonny pulled up a map of the intergalactic bank. "The bank's software system is backed up in three places: inside the bank itself, the Morrow, Inc. cloud, and an undisclosed location. Mrs. Morrow and you are the only people in this room who know where that undisclosed location is and so...."

"So that's the key, huh? You think I can just give it up, just like that?" I retorted

"I know where the undisclosed backup is," Angelica chimed in. "It's in the Foraxeum Galaxy, planet Grabiudom, in the city of Dihidribas."

She pulled it up in the hologram and sat back, basking in her glory.

"Well, this is great, we already have it!" Sunny blurted.

Mindy said what I had been thinking since the discussion started. "That's where it was backed up *last* Thursday. The backup location happens via an algorithm every hour, on the 18th minute, on the 34th second, if I remember correctly."

"You do, and it's virtually impossible to know where it is going to be backed up every hour." I said.

"This is going to be a hard nut to crack," Sunny said.

"Mindy, what do you think?" I asked. I don't often ask questions to which I don't know the answer. But this time I really didn't know. It was part of our fail-safe plan. Backup procedures for the bank are on a need-to-know basis, and for liability reasons I never needed to know; basically, no one needed to know the entire piece of the pie. Now we were attempting to predict or corrupt our algorithm, and we had designed it to ensure it could never be cracked.

"What do I think? Well, I think...."

"What was that? Did you guys hear that?" I whispered. "I think I just heard the system for the theater power up."

"Nobody should be here," Angelica whispered back.

The theater audience seats rotated. Without skipping a beat, everyone piled everything back into their backpacks. The seats continued to rotate, ever so slowly.

"If this is the end, I just want you to know, Sonny, that I always...." Angelica began.

"Cool it! Be cool, everyone just talk like normal," I said.

"What do you mean? What are we supposed to say?" Angelica asked.

I hadn't thought quick enough for this situation. I knew I should have taken more improv classes.

The theater seats kept rotating, until two flashlight beams caught us.

My sister cocked her radar gun. "I have it set to stun. I think."

"Put that away," I sternly whispered.

We couldn't make out who it was, but we heard a "We have a possible 1032 in progress at the Carousel of Progress Theater...." on the radio.

"Why, hello!" I shouted. "No '1032' here. We're simply a few humble actors rehearsing a new play we are working on."

"Mr. Tom Morrow, is that you?" the voice inquired. "What are you doing here in the middle of the night? Did you get the silent alarm that we got, too? Are these the criminals?!"

"No, no, no officer. Well...you see, my sister Angelica here, she is back from school and is showing us what it takes to do improv sketch theater comedy."

"I love improv comedy! I catch it all the time at that Comedy Warehouse; well, at least I used to," the unidentified officer wistfully stated.

"Right. Well, we better get on with our lesson here. Not sure about that alarm, maybe we triggered it accidentally, I am sure it must have been a mistake."

"Do you mind if we watch you perform a scene? It would be so much fun!" the other officer said.

"Why, it's no problem," Angelica stated like an idiot.

"What are you doing?! We need these officers to leave, we don't know improv," I whispered.

"Everyone knows how to improv. We all have it within ourselves. Everyone has thoughts that come to mind. It starts when we are children. The issue is, at a very young age our elders stop telling us to speak our minds and to stop thinking for ourselves. For improv, one must remove all filters, all preconceived notions," she lectured as she floated around the room.

"Whoa, that was...insightful," Sonny said.

"Maybe you really did learn something in school, Socrates!" I whispered.

"To get started all we need is a suggestion from one of you, out there in the audience. Go on, shout it out," she said.

Did she really know what she was doing? She signaled over Mindy, Sonny, and myself, and, in a huddle you'd see at a zongball game, gave us a crash course on improv comedy.

"Say yes and don't deny what anyone else says. Be whatever you want, endow others with things, avoid conflict, don't try to be funny."

"Seats!"

"Theater!"

"Stage!" the officers shouted.

"How about something that is unrelated to the room we are in?" she retorted.

"Police and criminals!"

"Mr. Tom Morrow!"

Sonny jumped in, motioning to the group to start the charade.

"Hello fellow criminals, we better get planning this heist." What was he thinking?

I attempted something. "No, we are planning a Christmas party, look at the tree and the presents!"

"Of course we are planning a heist! Friday night! The Intergalactic Bank," Angelica said. Why, I'll never know. She grabbed me closer. "Don't deny, never deny," she whispered.

I pulled her in even closer and whispered, "You're uninvited to the company picnic."

Mindy chimed in next. "Do you think it is safe to talk about the plan here, Dunny?"

"Dunny? Oh, right, Dunny! Yeah, let me pull up my holographic device here," Sonny stated with confidence.

"Aren't we a bit worried that Mr. Tom Morrow might hear? He is very powerful and has sources and resources all over the city!" I said, drawing a chuckle from our audience.

"No, there is nothing to worry about. He is probably golfing somewhere, or exploiting his workers," Angelica said, drawing a few hoots and laughs.

"Well, as you know, I am the Fox and I am the boss of you. So, I say we need to go somewhere safer," I stated.

"You're the Fox? That's the biggest laugh I've heard all night. The Fox is *twice* the person you are. You're a joke," Angelica retorted.

"Well now, it sounds like we better get to plan...."

"*Keep fighting!*" the officers shouted in unison.

"No, no, I believe the scene is now over. Thank you, gentlemen, for humoring us and being so polite, but we better get back to our lesson. It can be intimidating to know people are watching," I stated calmly.

"No, no, no, the scene must keep going until it reaches a climax. We have a good thing going here!" Angelica continued. "Here's the plan, we need to figure out that algorithm to get in to the banking software, Dindy, what do you got?"

Mindy shrugged and played along.

"I did an analysis of the algorithm looking for any kind of loophole. However, I had jumped ahead a bit, if we are going to hack into the bank system and...uh...steal money, we may not need there to be a backup at all. If there is a simultaneous software update to the code, that looks like it should be there, a safety patch, it would be able to track what is happening and create a backdoor for us to steal information or money as we wish, undetected over the entire system. We just need to know someone at Morrow, Inc. to go alo...."

"They would never do that over there. We have tried several times to turn their workers, but the Morrow folks are screened, double- and triple-checked for criminal history or tendencies of any kind," I said, attempting to slow the speed of the information being divulged. Had this really just happened? My wife telling these officers our secrets? Does it matter anymore? We own the bank; this was a solid plan.

"Absolutely, Fox. The folks at Morrow are great. I guess there really is no way to break into the bank. I am going to go home now," Sonny stated as he exited the screen door on set.

"Not so fast, Dunny. We need dirt in order to flip one of these workers,"Angelica said.

Mindy slapped down a file folder on the table. "I've got it right here in these files."

Sonny picked them up and pretended to read them.

"Look at this. Mr. Tom Morrow himself may be vulnerable! It looks like he's been protecting someone for many years."

"I wonder why that is? What do you think of that, Fox?"

"Well, maybe....", Angelica began.

"Excuse me, she was talking to *me*," I interrupted. "The reasons we protect one another in life, especially family, is love, compassion, perspective, and empathy. There are quintillions of beings around the galaxy, all of which have their own journey and their own understanding of right and wrong. It is all about perspective. Sometimes we are tough to the people we love, even though you may do things to protect them from causing irreparable harm. This love, this bond, this respect is something that needs continued nurturing. Even if they don't know it, this is something that exists, throughout the universe, and even for people like myself and Mr. Tom Morrow. If you don't fight for one another, there is no need to fight for anything."

Angelica gave me a big hug. She held me tightly.

The officers rang out with applause and hopped on the stage with us. "Wow! That was so *real*, it was like a real scene, and everything. Angelica, is it?" the taller of the two officers asked.

"Why, yes, yes, it is, and this is my *boyfriend*, Sonny. You may know him as a professional street fighter."

"Well, be that as it may, thanks for the show. We'll get that alarm all straightened out and be on our way," the other officer stated as they left.

We were able to talk freely once more.

"Tom, we're going to need you to sign off on this last-minute security patch," my wife stated.

"We can't just randomly do a security patch on a day's notice. We are going to need to attempt a hack at the system. It won't actually cause any harm, but we need to roll out a *patch* for it later tomorrow. We need the three-factor fail-safe to stay in place, therefore not causing any real issues, but we will need to scare the bank enough to alert us. This needs to be completely untraceable to us. But, we can't loop anyone else in on it either."

"With Sonny's help, I should be able to create this thing. Mindy, can you work on the dummy patch? Angelica, can you try not to mess up this plan?"

"I think this will work," Sonny stated.

We left the theater and headed to our condo to execute our plan. While Sonny was a musical crooner, he was also an expert in proxy routing, which would be the key to the first phase of the plan. I won't bore you with the details, but it was really quite simple. We needed a virus that would be caught but not tracked. It needed to get deep enough into the system to raise concern, but not enough concern. We wanted it to look like it was going to do something, but it actually wouldn't. It would simply go in there and flag an alarm to trigger an intrusion. The virus could't be a polymorphic. We just needed it to be detected. It would be too complicated to do a boot sector virus due to the fail-safes.

Sonny and I worked for hours and finally reached the right file type. It was small, a resident virus. It was something that wouldn't be traceable due to our proxy server that was linked and tri-routed through four different sectors of our system. I can't divulge too much more, for the protection of our customers at the bank.

We needed to act fast. The virus would had to be detected this morning to get a patch out tomorrow night. We woke up Mindy and Angelica to monitor our actions to be double sure; measure twice, cut once. We reviewed the details. Mindy took a full look and gave it the thumbs up. Sonny took the honors of hitting *execute* on the keyboard. "Here goes nothin," he said.

We tracked its progress, and got the alert that it had made its way into the system. We had executed step one. It was about 3:00 am. I would need to sleep a few winks this night, for I knew it was going to be a white-knuckle ride in the coming days. I woke up a few hours later, and turned on my home work computer. I logged on to the Morrow, Inc. intranet. I had to act normal. I couldn't slip up and have our IT folks know I was attempting to look for something I shouldn't know was there.

By midday, I had my direct reports meeting: chief technology officer, chief operating officer, chief financial officer, and yes, the most talented chief innovention officer any company in the galaxy had, my wife, Mindy. We had gone through our normal rundown. The CTO had yet to mention the breach. I had to be quick on my feet. I had to *improvise*.

"Brandon, is there anything else going on today, perhaps in the cyber-security sector? Any breaches we should discuss?"

"We had a minor breach this morning at the Tomorrowland Intergalactic Bank. It was caught immediately, and we reported it to the police and are attempting to trace it."

"I know, that's why I'm asking," I bluffed. "What are we doing about this?"

"The breach was relatively benign. We are running analysis and should have a patch sometime late next week."

"Word will get out, it always does. We need a patch tonight, we need to address it," Jennifer, our chief operating officer, interrupted. She was right.

"I know that is a tight deadline. Jennifer, can you handle the press? Mindy, can you help out Brandon's team if they need it?"

"I think Brandon's team can handle this one," Mindy replied. She was good; lots of plausible deniability here.

"We need to get this fixed ASAP. Mindy, let's get this resolved," Jennifer added.

"I agree. I will leave it with you all to do what is best, but we need that patch tonight," I said.

This was working perfectly. I was confident and leading again. However, there was one little hitch from Brandon, one loose end that needed tying up. He stayed after the meeting was over and asked me point blank.

"Sir, how did you know about that breach? I had it under control."

I had many options here. I needed him to save face. I needed him to know I had his back, and know that I had his trust so he had mine. Lesson to everyone reading this, it is never good to humiliate your coworkers. It wasn't a humiliation, but he was feeling a little heat. I decided to play it cool.

"Brandon, you know when something happens in this company that could damage the long-term viability, it is my job to know, and I have friends in all types of places." That was true,.but not this time.

"It was the police commissioner, wasn't it?" he asked. I gave him the straightest face I could possibly give him.

"I can't tell you my sources, Brandon, but I do have full faith and confidence in your team, especially since this is described as *benign*. I'll do my best to keep Jennifer and Mindy out of the situation, but would you let me know a status update before you leave tonight?"

"Absolutely, sir."

It really can be that easy to manage a team and get them to assist in hacking their own company. That's why you need to ensure that those you entrust with absolute power are honorable, honest, and trustworthy. You can see with this tale that even the most trustworthy crime-fighters may be up to no good. In this situation I was hoping I was doing the right thing, even if it took a little wrong to do it. The meeting was long over as I pondered these concepts in my office. Was I selling out my father's legacy?

A few minutes went by when I got an alert on my phone.

"Mr. Morrow, Mr. Tom Morrow. Please contact Mr. Johnson in the control tower to confirm your flight to the moon."

The police may have been making a few connections after all. I grabbed a Morrow cheeseburger at the Tomorrowland Terrace cafeteria downstairs and headed to the PeopleMover for my short trip to the control tower. There they were. The governor and the commissioner ready to divulge the latest.

"Mr. Tom Morrow, thank you for coming on such short notice. We got wind of the attempted hack this morning at the...." Commissioner Mitchel began.

"Intergalactic Bank, yes, yes, and my *top* people are on it right now investigating it. This kind of thing does happen. Why did you bring me all the way over here?" I asked, playing dumb.

"We think it may have been the Fox. Our cyber investigation team has traced the proxy a few degrees back to one that was linked to another hack a few months ago. We can't trace it beyond that, but with the Fox in town, we think it is related."

Based on this, it looks like Sonny had been working with Angelica for a while now.

"Wow, that's a good lead. I will personally ensure that we send out a patch as soon as possible, and we will send you everything your team needs to track this thing. I have top people on it. I do have one request, though. Would you kindly buy us a little time with the press?"

The governor stared at his computer screen intently. "Rumors are starting to spread on MorrowBook. We will do our best, but you better move quick on this patch."

"Thank you, Governor, and I assure you I will do everything I can to stop the Fox if they are up to something," I said.

Things were getting real. Without skipping a beat, I got an alert from Jennifer, my trusty chief operating officer. It was the press; they wanted a statement from me. The press had already gotten word that it was the Fox. We needed to circle the wagons, before this thing blew up in our faces. I told Jennifer to buy us some more time and that we would release a statement later that afternoon. I pinged the team to meet at our house in Morrow Tower.

Angelica, Mindy, and Sonny had assembled rather quickly. I didn't hesitate. I had to lay it all out there. "Sonny, you messed up! They've traced this to the Fox."

"That's not possible, I used a...." he began.

"You used the same proxy server you used a few months ago to help Angelica out with some other scheme," I curtly stated.

"It's not traceable."

"It is, and they did. At least to the Fox. They have a link, and we need to batten down the hatches. This hack is getting too much attention. We need to distract everyone from our trail."

"We could fake a robbery," Mindy stated. "I've been tracking the progress of the patch. They are looking to send it out around midnight tonight. While our dummy patch goes out, the heist could be happening."

"I don't like it. It's too risky and reckless."

"I'll do it," Sonny proclaimed.

"I'll do it, too. We're both needed for this," my sister added.

"Mindy, do you also want to risk your life?" I asked.

"I can't. I have the clearance to monitor the patch."

Angelica and Sonny stayed behind to review plans of the bank, while I went back to Morrow, Inc. to do a bit of damage control. I called Brandon in to get an update about the patch. It went very smoothly. He had his top people dissecting the hack. They had no leads, and knew as much as the police did, which wasn't much. With the patch release set for midnight, I now had something to report to the media to calm the masses. I needed this story squashed like a bug. We couldn't let the press get this out there and spook the criminals who were bound to make their transfers. It had to seem like business as usual. Jennifer asked again for some kind of statement to give the press. I obliged and held a quick conference call with the local reporters. I began my improvised speech:

"Hello, everyone. It has come to my attention that you have all been alerted about a *minor* glitch we had in our software today. This is something that happens all the time, sometimes every day. There is no story here. We have traced the benign breach and will have a patch sent out by the end of day. I assure you this is something that happens *all* the time, and is a normal part of cyber security."

I had Jennifer and Brandon on the phone line to back up my claim. They did, and it worked. The press found that there was no drama here, a minor occurrence. The police knew more, and we had to continue the heist as planned. Things would move quickly from here on out.

Brandon reported to me that the patch would be ready to go by the early evening, but would be released at midnight during the nightly turnover. Mindy had the dummy patch ready to go, and had switched the file over. That plan was all set, and it was time for the heist operation.

It was supposed to be straightforward, roughly around the time of the overnight patch. A perfect distraction, get in and get out, look as if they were thwarted before it was too late. We did the cliché thing and hovered nearby in our make-shift command center. Mindy was monitoring the patch via a double proxy, and I was monitoring the police signals from the heist. Sunny and Angelica ran toward the bank's backdoor entrance. The police had thought the Fox had taken a retinal scan of one of the bank managers who had been staying at the Hover Hotel the past week, so we used a hack that would corroborate that story. Within moments, Sonny and Angelica were in. We owned the bank video software, and ensured it was kept on a loop. They huddled in the main bank vault, sur-rounded by trillions of dollars.

They were alone, but managed to leave their radios on.

"Thank you, Sonny, for supporting me in all of this," my sister said.

"It is my pleasure. You have always had a way of bringing the best and the worst out of people."

"I'm tired of these games, I want to be together." It took me everything to not interrupt.

"The minute I said 'yes' to you months ago, you already had my heart," he replied.

Now I don't know what happened moments after that, but a deafening silence was heard on the radio. I was happy for them reconnecting, I really was. When we are honest with our feelings, only then can we truly live.

Just when I thought everything was going to plan, Mindy laid it on me. Our phony patch didn't go through. She did a quick search on our email severs and found out that a low-level software engineer noticed that the wrong file was set to update into the system due to an incorrect file size, another sloppy mistake that I would never mention to my wife.

"This was a sloppy mistake, Tom. It was my fault."

"How do we fix it?"

"Sonny needs to trigger the alarm, and we need to manually enter the phony patch. I can make the tweaks, but you're going to need to run it into the system manually."

"I really need to run in there?" I asked, knowing the answer.

She made the minor adjustments to the patch, and I raced to the backdoor using the bank manager's eye scan to enter. Sonny triggered the alarm on cue to set the distraction. I encountered Angelica who was in the vault and pleaded with her to leave in the escape hover car before it was too late. She disregarded my plea, of course, a move I did appreciate in the moment.

The alarm was wailing, and we penetrated each barrier, wall and lock, quickly with one hack after another. I demanded Mindy and Sonny leave the scene, as there was no need for them to get roped into this anymore. They complied promptly, and we made it to the computer core of the bank.

I took out my jump-drive and inserted it into the computer, seamlessly replacing the patch with our tracking software. We quickly reversed our steps through the bank, wiping out the memory of any door ever being opened.

Meanwhile, the police were swarming on the Fox. Angelica was tracking them on the radar. We were cornered on all sides. I activated my rocket boots, held onto Angelica, and blasted through the corridors toward the basement for an escape through the sewers. We landed by the hatch and I attempted to unlock it. We heard voices of police echoing through the halls. We were trapped.

This was too much. We had one way out, my fail-safe. I broke out Mindy's latest invention, which was no larger than a watch, and demanded that Angelica hold my hand.

"Why?" She asked.

"Trust me, and close your eyes. It's the only way."

She squeezed my hand tight, and I brought her in for a much-needed hug as I locked in the coordinates and pressed the launch button. We were instantly teleported to my condo. Angelica gave Sonny and Mindy a big hug and regained her composure.

"What was that?"

Mindy gave her a knowing look.

"If we are going to capture all these criminals throughout the galaxy, we're going to need a bigger team," I cheekily stated.

I waved my hand in the house, giving the system the signal to activate the Wonder Beacon, and holograms of my dear friends appeared.

"Auntie Gravity, checking in."

"Robo-Newz reporting for duty."

"Timekeeper, clocking in"

"Captain EO, *OOOOOOOW!*"

About the Authors

Patrick Kling is a former Disneyland cast member and lifelong theme park enthusiast. By night he is an author of the Stories from the Magic Kingdom series, and by day he works professionally in the theme park design industry, helping create themed experiences around the world.

Follow Patrick on Instagram @ipatsk to stay connected with his theme park adventures, CrossFit motivation, and humorous antics.

Kristen Waldbieser is an Orlando native and former Walt Disney World cast member who spent her life as an avid Disney fan. Kristen studied creative writing at the University of Central Florida, where she had her first short story published in the college literary magazine.

Follow Kristen on Instagram @kristen.lee.w to stay connected with her theme park photography, her dog Gus Gus, and volunteer work.

Stay connected with the series by following on Facebook and Instagram @StoriesFromTheMagicKingdom.

Get the latest updates, and share your thoughts and photos by using the hashtag #SFTMK to be featured on our social media channels.

And don't forget to visit:
www.storiesfromthemagickingdom.com

ABOUT THEME PARK PRESS

Theme Park Press publishes books primarily about the Disney company, its history, culture, films, animation, and theme parks, as well as theme parks in general.

Our authors include noted historians, animators, Imagineers, and experts in the theme park industry.

We also publish many books by first-time authors, with topics ranging from fiction to theme park guides.

And we're always looking for new talent. If you'd like to write for us, or if you're interested in the many other titles in our catalog, please visit:

www.ThemeParkPress.com

• •

Theme Park Press Newsletter

Subscribe to our free email newsletter and enjoy:

- ◆ Free book downloads and giveaways
- ◆ Access to excerpts from our many books
- ◆ Announcements of forthcoming releases
- ◆ Exclusive additional content and chapters
- ◆ And more good stuff available nowhere else

To subscribe, visit www.ThemeParkPress.com, or send email to newsletter@themeparkpress.com.

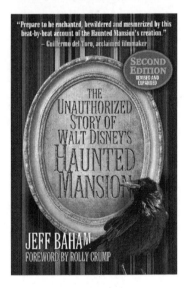

Read more about these books
and our many other titles at:

www.ThemeParkPress.com

Made in the USA
San Bernardino, CA
19 September 2018